COALESCE

A PHOENIX DRAGON NOVEL 02

MAX ANDREN

ANCOR PRESS

A Phoenix Dragon Prequel 02: Coalesce
Copyright © 2017 by Max Andren/ AnCor Press

Cover: Deranged Doctor Designs
Interior: AnCor Press
ISBN: 978-1-944599-13-3

Sign up for my—Spam-FREE Newsletter for New Release Notifications.
Max Andren: Magic and Mythos.

http://maxandren.com/magic-and-mythos-book-link/

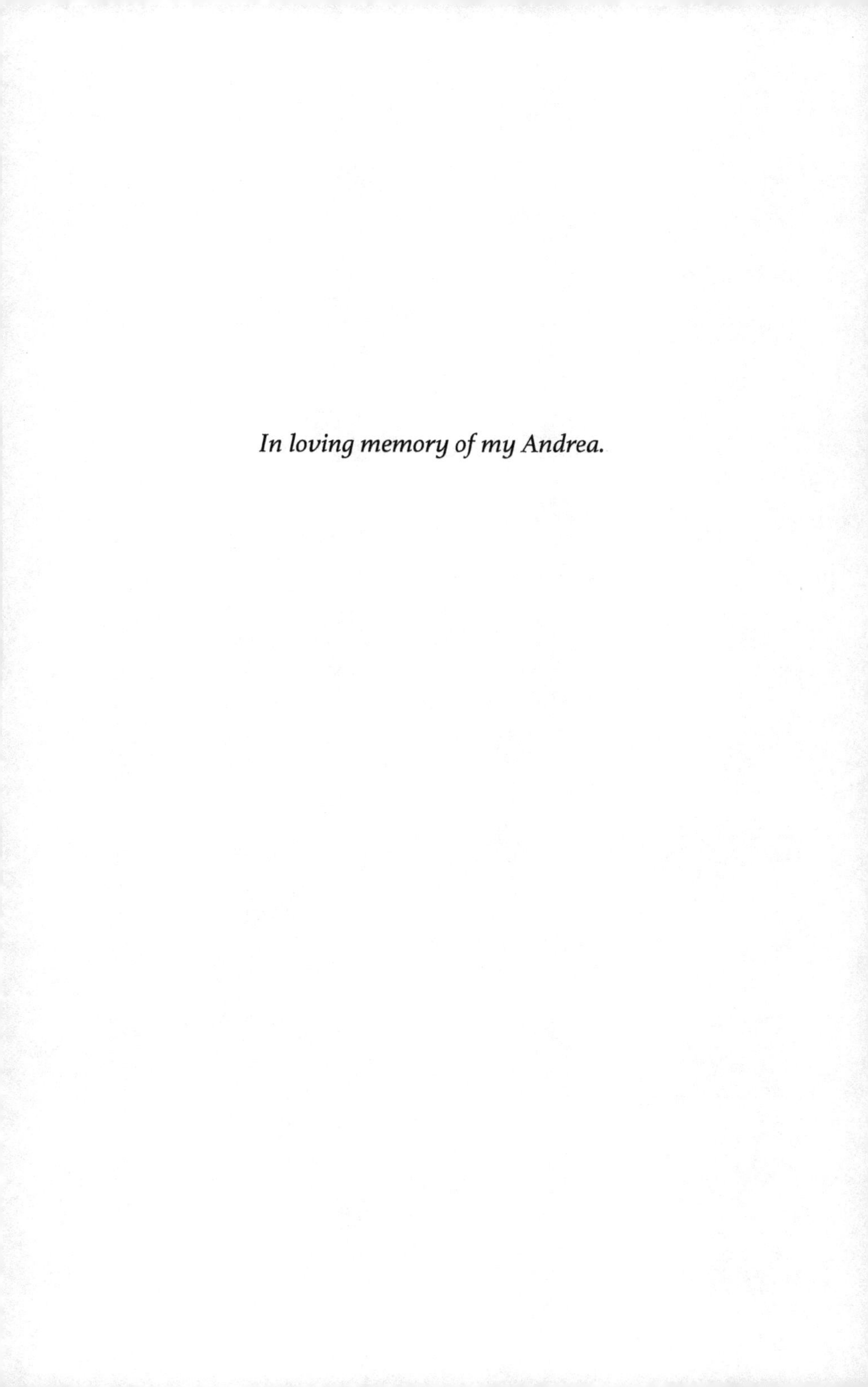

In loving memory of my Andrea.

They said I was the last true Phoenix and the dragon spoken about in legend and prophecy. They said I would be the one to bring the fragmented clans back together.

I said, *"I accept all that I am and all that I will become. I am the last true Phoenix."*

It had all began when I chose to do the inexplicable and embrace their idea as truth and that decision would echo through the rest of my life.

My declaration had been a mere formality for what would unfold regardless of my acceptance. I still harbored doubts as to the veracity of the last true Phoenix, but I would own that premise, if for no other reason than to help my new dragon family. I would aid them, and myself, in the plight against our mortal enemy—the drampires.

It was one of the defining moments of my life, though I often thought, 'what the hell have I done?'

It had been several years since I'd been rescued from my asylum hell and that question had plagued my mind incessantly—along with about a bazillion other questions that had no discernible answers.

What I'd *said* that day and what I *felt* today were not one and the same.

Today, I felt like a fraud!

My life had certainly improved since my rescue and yet, you could take the girl out of the asylum, but you couldn't take the dank asylum out of the girl.

I was strong and resilient, I had to be, I'd died and became Renascent. But that didn't make me immune to the doubts that plagued my mind or the emotions of unworthiness that strove to undermine the foundation I was creating.

I was now a full-fledged Phoenix Dragon, but nothing was ever as simple as it would seem and my life was far from simple or mundane.

"Do you feel that?" I asked Cipriano with my mind.

We were in dragon-form flying over Lake of the Ozarks searching for the perfect location to build sanctuary. It was easy to see how the serpentine-shaped lake had garnered its nickname, *The Magic Dragon*. It was beautiful and ironic.

The lake itself had twelve hundred miles of shoreline and was lined with lush trees and vegetation that were interspersed with rocky cliffs and sandy beaches. The varied terrain hugged the water's edge for over ninety miles through central Missouri.

Somewhere below, in the vastness that was the Ozarks, we would build sanctuary and set down roots for the dragon race to grow and thrive—together, I prayed.

Our search today would be delayed by whatever was pulling at me. The compulsion to investigate right now was overwhelming.

"I feel...a vague sense of unease?" Cipriano answered with uncertainty.

"Something or someone is in a tremendous amount of pain and it's coming from that small lake over there," I said, and took off in the direction I'd indicated.

The noxious pain was so compelling, it forced me to spontaneously shift.

My less than graceful landing was, thankfully, cushioned by wild grass. The soft thud of my booted feet, was immediately followed by a loud grunt and a gasping wheeze, as I dropped the rest of the way to the ground, my bent knee jammed into my diaphragm.

Glancing at Cipriano, I rolled my eyes at his superior landing—show off.

Despite my shortness of breath, I jumped up to follow the empathic pain that resonated through me in diminishing waves. This visceral connection was my only guide and I was acutely attuned to its rapidly fading source.

It pulled me through thick vegetation that hid ankle-rolling rocks and thorn-laden locust trees—which ripped at my skin through my jeans. Why couldn't I have landed in a more hospitable area, like the one where I was headed?

Once I reached the water's edge, I searched along the shore for anything that could be the source of the pain. Finding nothing, I turned and walked towards my right, where Cipriano searched through the dark woods and it was in that moment that a pair of glistening wings caught my attention.

At first glance, I thought they might have belonged to a butterfly or perhaps a large dragonfly. Could this be the source of the pain that resonated like a beacon? An insect?

Dropping to my knees, I was unprepared for what I found.

A faery!

I should be used to the fact that there were other supernatural creatures running about besides dragons and drampires, but I wasn't. Cipriano had once intimated we weren't alone by quoting Shakespeare, "There are more things in heaven and earth."

But a faery?

Brutally abused and discarded like trash, she was laying crumpled and unnaturally still between the edge of the lake and the dark woods. My aura was vibrating with the need to heal and tentacles of my essence were reaching for her.

I gently lifted her up and cradled her limp body in my hand. When I did so, I noticed to my horror that her wings had been ripped from her back and were laying on the ground next to her.

And, she was dying.

I could feel her heart stuttering against my bloody palm. Her breaths were shallow and stridorous, as she tried to breathe through the swelling that was obstructing her throat and airway.

"What do you have there?" Cipriano asked when he saw me drop to the ground.

"I don't know. A faery?" I said, and showed him my hand where she was laying.

I barely felt her weight and thought she couldn't have weighed more than a hummingbird.

"They often travel in packs, but we won't see the others, not unless they want to be seen. She looks bad, Charani."

Cipriano used his index finger to move her long silver, lavender and black hair from covering her delicate features. The bright sunlight exposed her grievous injuries and they were a shocking contrast to her pale, pearlescent skin.

Cipriano looked at me and our eyes connected. The rage blazing in his was undoubtedly mirrored in mine, as we were both feeling the red haze of it.

Her face had been battered and was covered in dark purple bruises. Both of her eyes were swollen shut and discolored. Her pale lips were swollen and split. Finger marks of dark purple and red, marred the skin around her neck—where evidently, someone had attempted to strangle her to death.

"Can you heal her?"

"I'm going to try."

The white light of healing from my aura and the blue iridescence from my dragon essence surrounded her little body seeking to heal her injuries. I reached through the haze of her pain, to find the core of the little faery.

When we finally connected, she was about to cross over to the the other side. I had to intervene fast or she'd die.

"I can help you, but only if you are willing to accept the gift," I told her with my mind.

"Yes..." She said, in weak reply.

"Her heart stopped!"

I quickly tethered her soul to mine.

"Did you reach her?"

We both knew what he was asking.

Her color quickly faded to grey.

"Drink of my essence, little faery, and be risen. Be Renascent!" I implored aloud.

Mind to mind and heart to heart, my essence bathed her soul in the chance to be reborn and to live again.

Her aura wavered, indecisive—losing all of its color and vibrance.

I lifted her closer to watch her delicate face. She was so dainty. Her pointed ears were peeking out from under her beautiful, tricolored hair. Her up-turned nose was crooked and swollen.

She was dying right before my eyes.

"Come on, little one. Drink and be reborn!"

Nothing. I felt nothing at all, no response from her—just a void. I looked at Cipriano and he shook his head. He felt it too.

I'd lost her.

Her choice had been made and she passed over to the other side. Her injuries must have been irreparable and her pain far too debilitating to overcome.

Tears clouded my vision, which was a rarity. I'd learned the hard way not to show emotion, but for Dreah's sake, I'd been working to overcome that flaw.

It made me so angry and so sad to know that her life had been taken by someone else. Her delicate wings brutally ripped from her body. I couldn't fathom that kind of hate and anger.

A tear escaped to splash onto my little faery, bathing her in my remorse and sadness.

"I'm going to drown if you don't stop the waterfall pouring from your eyes, My Lady," whispered a weak, but lyrical voice through my mind.

2

My eyes flew open.

No drowning the faery, I thought with a smile and reached up to wipe the tears from my face. She looked so much better. Her complexion was no longer ashen grey and her aura was gaining a small measure of color and vibrance.

The essence of my dragon and the healing of my aura were working their magic. We could see that her injuries were subsiding. Score one for the good guys.

The swelling about her face and neck had dramatically decreased making it possible for her eyes to be open. She sat up in my hand and pulled her knees to her chest, then turned to look at Cipriano.

"My Lord," she said in greeting.

He answered her address by saying, "Please, just Cipriano."

She nodded her head in acquiescence and said, "Lovely to make your acquaintance, just Cipriano. I'm just Violet."

The corners of Cipriano's attentive grey eyes crinkled when he smiled at her joke.

Violet turned and focused her exotic, upwards-slanted eyes on me. I was mesmerized by their ethereal purple hue. She was too beautiful to be of this world, I thought, and I realized she probably wasn't.

As we took each other's measure, I could see that the pain was slowly fading from the depths of her eyes.

"I'm Charani," I said, and then asked, "How are you feeling?"

"That's a good question, My Lady. I'm better than I was just a bit ago," she paused, shrugging her shoulders and tilting her head left and then right, "and yet, I'm not quite as I was…before," she answered hesitantly.

"You're definitely breathing better and your color has improved," I observed.

"Oh!" She exclaimed, "I think I'm healing quite well. Pray forgive me, I thought you meant to inquire how I was feeling after you brought me back to life with your Phoenix," she said, surprising me.

I wondered how she knew that. I wasn't exactly waving my freak flag about and announcing that I was a Phoenix Dragon. However, in offering her my essence, we *had* connected on a deeper plane—the place where the soul resides and where all and yet, nothing is known.

"But, to answer your question, I'm feeling much better. Though I have to admit to feeling a bit itchy where my wings were torn away," she said, standing up to scratch her back.

"Here, let me help you," I said, but before I could rub her back, I saw the reason for her itchiness.

"Violet, can your wings regenerate?"

"I honestly do not know. I've never heard of another faery being gifted with wing regeneration. That's why people rip them off in the first place," she said solemnly, but then asked with hesitant, yet hopeful awe, "Truly, they are sprouting anew?"

"Truly. Don't you feel them pushing through?"

She nodded her head and grimaced. "Oh...I do now," she said, then whispered, "and 'tis quite painful."

I could feel her pain, as her new wings pushed their way through the mended skin of her back. I sent my aura to surround her again and the relief was evident on her face.

"Violet, how did you come to be here today? Who abused you so grievously?"

Sadness and betrayal flashed through our connection and that was all I needed to know.

"Are you in danger now? Would you like to come live with us and eventually at sanctuary?"

"What is sanctuary?" She asked, hope gleaming in her eyes.

"We are creating a dragon colony of sorts. A place where

various dragon clans can come together to live and thrive. So far it's just an idea. But you can live with us in the city, until it's all finished," I offered.

Violet nodded her head, though not really in answer, but in acknowledgement and acceptance.

"Oh, Goddess!" She exclaimed suddenly and shot off my hand when her wings had fully sprouted.

She flew around Cipriano and I, getting a feel for her new wings. They were beautiful and different from the mutilated ones on the ground. The old ones were smaller and more translucent.

Her new wings were just as delicate, so that her frame could handle their weight, but they were much larger, like that of a butterfly. Her wings were a translucent silver at their insertion point and transitioned in an ombré-like fashion, from lavender to black. The ends were tipped in dragon blue and there were pools of my Phoenix red staggering along the edges..

I didn't know what to make of that. A Phoenix Faery? Weren't Fae already immortal? She'd died from her injuries, but had risen, Renascent. Perhaps she would become a Phoenix.

Violet landed by her bloody wings and knelt down next to them. We watched, as she bowed her head and then with a wave of her hands, her wings disappeared, as if they'd never been.

She turned, opened and closed her wings, and said demurely, "Thank you, My Lady."

Her words were accompanied by a curtsy to rival all curtsies. She performed the courtly gesture, as if she were wearing a beautiful ball gown and not a bloody dress that hung in tatters on her delicate frame.

She reminded me of a queen before her court—gracious and regal all at once.

"There are others coming this way," Violet said before she flew up to my face to stare into my crystal blue eyes with her ethereal purple ones.

"I'm not ready to meet anyone else. May I rest upon your skin and heal?"

I nodded my head, yes, despite the strange nature of her request.

"Will you move your long red and black hair to the side?"

I grabbed my hair and moved it aside as she requested, and exposed the skin of my neck and shoulder. She landed there with her bare feet and once our skin touched, Violet was able to change.

When she shifted from a faery of flesh-and-blood, to a faery of colorfully rendered ink, like a tattoo upon my shoulder—a stinging sensation accompanied the transition. Once settled, she was able to move along my skin and wrapped herself around my left side.

I could feel her emotions and felt her revulsion to the skin between my shoulder blades, where the dark magic glyph had been etched. I couldn't blame her for that, I hated it too.

I wondered if we would be able to communicate when she was this way and asked her with my mind.

"Yes, My Lady, we can. We shall be able to share and sense each other's emotions too."

3

Our family landed in the clearing and by unspoken agreement, Cipriano and I chose not to tell them about Violet. We didn't like keeping secrets, but we would honor Violet's desire not to meet anyone.

Dreah Xavier jumped down from Tarrin's dragon back and made her way over to me. The spring sunshine bathed her long auburn hair with beautiful golden highlights. When I looked at Dreah, it was hard to remember that she wasn't the age she appeared to be, especially with her old soul shining from her amber eyes.

She had always been mature for her age, but now she looked to be around eighteen years of age—which we all knew wasn't the case. After I'd rescued her and given her some of my dragon essence, she'd initially matured at a normal rate. However, over the last several years we'd noticed an acceleration in the aging process. Fortunately, that seems to have settled back down to a normal rate of maturation.

Dreah had handled the whole thing with grace and acceptance, as if her aging was the most natural of things and, perhaps it was. We had no way of knowing how she would have matured on her own and without the essence of my Phoenix Dragon changing her genetic expression.

Dreah walked around the small clearing, as did the rest of the family. And now that I wasn't frantically searching for the source of the empathic pain I had been slammed with, I could appreciate the area around us.

We were surrounded by dense trees and near the edge of a crystal clear lake. The earthy scent of new vegetation was intoxicating and was carried on a warm spring breeze. The wooded area was lush with cedar, white oak, elm, hickory and walnut trees, as well as those stupid locust trees and bushes with their needle-like thorns.

Cipriano and I had traveled to the Ozarks multiple times to find the right location for sanctuary. I was looking for an area that resembled the prophetic vision Dreah had shared with me years ago. We knew it would be difficult to find, though not impossible.

Once we narrowed the choices to three possibilities, we'd brought the family along to get their opinions. I wanted to see if any of them resonated with Dreah or felt similar to her vision. This area had not been one of the three choices.

Violet had led us here.

Today we'd driven the three hours to the Ozarks so that Dreah could accompany us. Once we were in a secluded location, she was placed upon the back of Tarrin's dragon.

Usually we travelled from Kansas City to the Ozarks disguised as large birds. This enabled us to hide in plain site preventing normals, humans without magic, from recognizing what we were when they looked to the skies above.

We were still in dragon form, just a smaller version, like my hatchling, though not quite that small. From a distance we resembled birds. .

I'd never forget the first time I shifted. Stressed over Mia fading, I'd recklessly thrown myself into that pool of power running through my dragon essence. I'd shifted into a hatchling small enough to fit in Cipriano's palm. I'd remained that way for hours because I couldn't shift back to my human form —I didn't know how.

It was fairly comical, especially when I'd spontaneously shift hours later. Naked and oblivious, I sat on the great room floor laughing until Isabella pointed out that I was sans clothes!

It was one of my favorite memories, despite being naked in front of everyone. Ian had placed his warm jacket around my shoulders and I'd left the room with my head held high.

Now that my Phoenix had been fully realized, I'd learned the in-and-outs of shifting to a more proper sized dragon. It was extremely useful, however, to have the ability to choose the size I wanted to be, depending on the situation. Or, I could just shift into my shadowed form, especially if stealth was needed.

I loved my little hatchling, as she represented where I'd been. I still feel like that little hatchling at times—confused and so unsure of myself and my place within this new world I was navigating.

"This is a beautiful spot and well away from normals," I commented to the family, once they joined us.

"Yes," Cipriano replied, "But close enough for shopping and supplies."

This particular spot felt like the right one.

"Dreah, what do you think of this area?"

When I looked in her direction, she nodded her head and replied, "If *ever* there was a place for the dragons to come together and be *lasting*—this would be the place."

That was several years ago and now we lived in the Ozarks full-time, though we still maintained the estate in Kansas City. We spent the intervening years planning, creating, and implementing my dream for sanctuary.

Fortunately, Cipriano had amassed a fortune over the centuries, so money wasn't a concern. However, before we started notifying various dragon clans about our Lake of the Ozarks sanctuary, we wanted everything to be in readiness.

We had no way of knowing how many dragons would eventually join us, but we would be prepared in any case. We owned a lot of land and could build as many homes as were needed. Plus, there were caves everywhere throughout this area and the Interior Highlands, so there should be plenty of options.

Sanctuary was located far enough out of the way, that I wasn't too worried about the normals who lived locally. However, I was worried about detection by our enemies. Once word began to spread, there would be no way to keep our location a secret, even though we would try. After all, it was in our best interest to be secreted away from the drampires—a dream and an impossibility, that much I knew.

Sometimes, it's less painful not to dream at all.

4

Cipriano and I had reached out to the Ames de la Terra, or Souls of the Earth, for guidance in creating our Lake of the Ozarks sanctuary. They were a peaceable group of supernaturals located in Louisiana, outside of Rouen and throughout the Bisou Islands.

We wanted to emulate what they'd created for their brethren in the islands. There were various supernaturals living there, all in harmony and without strife—something we wanted for our culture. But, with the realization there were other supernatural creatures, every time I turned around, one would be waving their metaphorical hand at me in greeting.

There was so much to learn about this new world and where I fit in to its hierarchy.

Vampires existed, and they were blood-sucking and allergic to sunlight, though I'd seen a few that could tolerate diffused light. I'd also seen wolf and cat shifters, and witch familiars. And from what Violet had told me, Faery really did exist, though she wouldn't elaborate beyond the confirmation that it was real.

Cipriano told me that there were two camps in regards to the supernatural world. Those that believed normals were expendable and those who believed they were to be protected. It was obvious which camp the dragons and the drampires belonged to.

Drampires killed normals and my dragon brethren indiscriminately to feed their diabolic cravings for immortality. They had zero regard for human life or magical beings. Cipriano thought drampires could belong to a secret order of supernaturals called the Principes Noctis or the Rulers of the Night.

The Principes believed that normals were less than animals and should be treated as such. The Ministry governed all Principes and was founded by a leadership of nine supernaturals. They would stop at nothing to force normals to bow down before them in supplication.

Evil couldn't exist without its opposition and that was represented by the Ames. They'd been forced into combat with the Principes in order to protect normals.

At first, I'd thought we could relocate to Rouen and join the Ames de la Terra's fight against the Ministry, however based upon various scenarios I'd seen in Dreah's vision, I knew we needed to move to the Ozarks. Its lush terrain would be the perfect place to develop a dragon colony.

Shortly after we arrived to live at sanctuary full-time, we were surprised to have a small group of witches ask to join us. They sought peace and refuge from magical persecution. They told us that they ascribed to a different philosophy than their fellow witches and were forced to leave their coven.

That was the only explanation that was offered.

The Ames had vouched for the three of them and that was enough for me.

We welcomed them to sanctuary and it was fortunate that we did. The three witches, Dusky, Lyan, and their leader, Kestrel, have been incredibly helpful. They created a magical shield that deterred detection by normals.

When the locals approached the shield surrounding sanctuary, they would forget why they'd driven out of town in the first place and would turn around to go home. Unlike the dark magic used by drampires, the witches used a magical shield that made normals forget, rather than use repulsion and fear—white magic versus dark.

I was thankful they'd come to join us and for multiple reasons. The three witches, plus Isabella, Dreah, and I, were becoming extremely close. They adored Dreah and could teach her things that the family couldn't—like witchy things. Plus, they knew all about birthing children and that was our ultimate dream, to start the next generation of dragons here at sanctuary.

Now that all was ready, we just needed to convince the centuries-old clans to come to sanctuary. Relocation and renascence of the dragons was my first priority; whether I was up to the task was another thing altogether. Regardless of my doubts, Cipriano and I put a call out to the clans hoping to unite them in purpose.

It was disheartening to realize that the dragon race was a fraction of what it used to be. With drampires killing mates, dragons were losing their ability to procreate. We had to find a way to protect the mated couples, along with the rest of the dragon race.

We hoped the premise of safety in numbers would resonate with the leaders and they'd bring their clansmen, as well as their mated dragons, here to sanctuary—no more hiding.

Dreah's prophetic vision was the impetus for all my actions. I foresaw various scenarios played out within her mind. Some of these potential outcomes were unspeakably horrific. I would do whatever was necessary to ensure that the dragon clans survived the drampires' obsessive thirst for immortality.

The genocide had to be stopped before the dragon race was decimated to the point of extinction.

As a result, I felt a huge responsibility upon my shoulders, given I was, *the supposed*, last true Phoenix. But demons of doubt continually plagued my mind. It was hard to release those old feelings of worthlessness, but I tried—daily!

There was an influx of dragon leaders, coming and going from sanctuary, as we solidified plans for their relocation. They all conveyed their desire and willingness to work together to find a resolution to the drampire threat.

But nothing ever went as planned, no matter how well orchestrated and, actions spoke eloquently, where words were cheap.

5

Dragon clans from around the world were slowly migrating to the Ozarks and our sanctuary was steadily growing. We were a strong race, with unique and varied magical abilities, but from what Cipriano had told me, we were a culture that kept to itself.

My hope was to bring them back together as one united clan. If they were all in one central location, perhaps the dragons would feel protected and would be able to flourish and perhaps deliver a new generation of dragons. They had been living separately and scattered across the world for more centuries than imaginable, but that was changing.

Times change and we must change with them—or die. As such, this was a learning process for all of us. Regardless of how uncomfortable it proved to be, change was necessary —dire even.

Drampires had always coveted our immortality and would stop at nothing to have it, including genocide.

I was fairly new to the dragon culture and the concept of dragons working together was new to them. We would navigate this new inception together. Although there would be growing pains, we must put our culture ahead of our own preferences. But this concept would prove to be more difficult for some clansmen than others.

The pre-meetings with the first wave of clan leaders had given us an idea of how many clansmen would be coming and what their needs might be. We were able to accommodate each one as they arrived, since we'd been able to plan ahead of time. Their new homes were scattered all throughout the area.

We'd also created a central location at sanctuary and placed community buildings there. We wanted to offer a neutral place to gather and to get to know one another, yet they could still retreat to their homes and maintain that sense of isolation. We felt that was important for a positive transition.

Our home was near the hub of sanctuary, easily accessible and centrally located. We wanted to show our commitment to uniting the clans. If we were available and interacting with everyone, we hoped they would all follow suit. We couldn't afford to remain distant, not if our culture was to survive.

Things weren't exactly evolving at a rapid pace in that

regard. The clans were settling into their homes without issue, but they continued to maintain their distance from each other, so there hadn't been much interaction.

We heard from the leaders in weekly updates, but no one was doing anything to encourage their clansmen to interact with the others. In the last meeting I brought up protection at sanctuary.

"I think that one way we can foster interactions between the various clans would be in the creation of a dragon guard. This would bring various clansmen together in a singular purpose and require daily training sessions."

"I don't know if that would help," Geoffrey said, unconvinced at the possibilities.

He was centuries old, like most of those in today's meeting. Geoffrey was also one of the more vocal and least likely to embrace change. Though, to give him credit, he did move his people here, so that's something.

I had to remind myself that these men were not *men*, but dragons and stubborn as hell!

They had centuries of status quo, but death lies in that direction and they have to realize that they can no longer afford to remain stagnate.

"I really feel that if we give them a mutual goal, they will be united in that. Plus with the new sense of purpose and drive, hopefully that will spill over to their people when they return home after a patrol or training session," I told them, hoping to sway them to my way of thinking.

"I'm with Geoffrey on this, I don't think having the different dragons patrolling together will work and might actually have the opposite effect. How can they trust each other, when they've never worked together?" Alain replied.

When they refused to listen to my suggestions, Cipriano added his support for my plan. We didn't share my entire history with them, but they all knew I was the supposed last true Phoenix Dragon and the only dragon to have been born in the past several centuries.

"Geoffrey and Alain, no worries. Please don't feel as if you need to send your clansmen to participate in our program. The rest of you though, if you want your clans to be represented within our elite guard, then I suggest you seek out your most eligible dragons and send them to us," Cipriano told the other clan leaders.

He continued on to say, "Charani has devised a plan for the development of an elite dragon guard. These talented dragons will represent each of your clans. They will be responsible for the safety of all the clansmen here at sanctuary."

Check and mate!

How could they *not* want their men or women to participate. I sent Cipriano a wave of gratitude through our connection.

We recruited the dragons that had expressed interest to their clan leaders in patrolling sanctuary and becoming a part of our elite guard. We charged them with organizing themselves into rotating shifts to patrol the vast area that encompasses sanctuary and the surrounding area as well.

Tarrin and Tauric were instrumental in helping with the new guard. They organized training sessions and scouting maneuvers. The guards were the most active and engaged of all the dragons. I prayed my idea would work and that this elite guard would encourage interactions among the rest of the clans.

After talking with the family, we decided to implement an additional defense program for anyone who was interested. Tarrin and Tauric would lead that as well, but Dreah and I would be involved. There would be weekly lessons and we hoped this would entice the female clansmen into participating.

We were making slow progress forward with very small steps, but at least we were steadily moving in the right direction and towards the ultimate goal of clan unity.

It was a strange dichotomy I found myself in. I was held in awe by the clans for being the last true Phoenix and yet, they remained distrustful of me and my motives. It was a rejection of sorts and far too reminiscent of my parents—when they made me, a little girl thrown away.

My biological parents gave me away and my adoptive ones —well, they just plain threw me away.

I tried not to dwell on these emotions—acceptance or rejection, because neither would do me any good. I couldn't change what I was or where I'd been, but I was learning to accept both.

My family was at the estate in Kansas City taking a much-needed break from sanctuary. There was so much to do with settling the dragon clans that were relocating to the Ozarks, that we rarely had time for private family gatherings. This was a nice reprieve.

Dreah asked to have a family meeting, so after dinner we all gathered in the great room.

"Where'd Dreah run off to?" Ian asked.

He was sitting on the couch with Isabella nestled between his wide-spread legs so he could rub her shoulders. Her head was hanging forward and tipping left and right, so that Ian could hit just the right spot. It looked heavenly and she was clearly enjoying every moment of his attention.

"She ran to grab something from her room. She should be back at any moment," I told them.

"I'm back," Dreah announced, as she came bouncing into the room.

She had an expression on her face that was hard to place, but she was excited about something, that much was clear. Time would tell, so I would be patient and wait for her to reveal just what she was glowing about. Cipriano looked my way and nodded, conveying that he had noticed the same thing.

"As you all know," she began, excitement making her breathless, "I've been working with the witches at sanctuary. They've taught me a lot about their culture and about magic, including how to cast various types of spells."

"Dreah, they do have names you know," I teased.

"I know. It's just easier to lump them all together," she replied with a cheeky grin and continued, "I had a vision awhile ago which compelled me to make something and to make it using a bit of magic. See?"

She held out her hands, as if to show us something, but her hands appeared to be empty and I told her as much.

"I know!" She squealed, "Isn't it just grand?"

"What's grand, Dreah?" Cipriano asked, just as confused as the rest of us.

"You can't see what I'm holding in my hand? Is that what you are telling me?"

We all answered that we couldn't see anything.

"What about now?" She asked, waving her left hand over her right, as she whispered something simultaneously.

As she did so, seven amulets appeared and were dangling from her right hand. They reminded me of Hulbetto's Amulet of the Dead that I'd destroyed, releasing the collective trapped within. Hulbetto had used it to fuel his immortality with the essence of my dragon brethren.

"What do you have there, Dreah?" I asked with trepidation.

"Before I answer, will you all trust me with a strange request?"

We all answered that we would and without reservation. We trusted her implicitly, just as she trusted us. We were family—plain and simple.

"Come over here then, if you would?" She asked.

She grabbed a charcoal grey woolen throw off the back of the sofa and threw it onto of the coffee table, before placing the silver amulets on top. Some were more masculine appearing than others, with wider leather cords and thicker silver.

Each amulet was about the size of Cipriano's thumb and intricately molded, and had a glossy black stone at the center. Dreah pulled a sharp looking knife from her pocket and laid it next to the amulets.

"Dreah, please explain why it looks like we are about to start a drampire reaping ceremony?" I asked with a bit of humor, but in all seriousness.

"I know," she said simply, but filled with emotion, "just trust me, okay?"

"What do you need us to do?" Cipriano and I asked at the same time.

We all watched as she poked her index finger with the sharp blade and proceeded to place a drop of her blood on each stone.

"The stone will absorb my blood. It's similar to what drampires do, yet not at all. I need each of you to do the same."

We each did as she requested and knew that she must have a good reason to ask us to do so. Once finished, Dreah waved her hands over the amulets. They briefly glowed and swirled with the blue iridescence of our dragon essence and then turned back to stone. The color of each stone had changed. Now they had a marbled blue-and-black appearance, instead of just a glassy-black.

Dreah picked up one of the feminine amulets and slipped the cord over her neck and the whole thing disappeared.

"Where'd your amulet go?" I asked.

"I'll answer you in a minute," she replied, then handed each one of us an amulet.

"Now, slip your amulet over your head," she directed.

We did as she asked. Each amulet disappeared from view, but when I looked down at mine, I could see that it was still there.

"I can still see mine," I said.

We looked to Dreah, who was smiling from ear to ear, happy with her accomplishment.

"*Now,* I will explain. First, I wanted to be sure the amulets would disappear from view and they did. Yet, each person can still see their own. That part worked out just as I'd thought," she said.

I noticed her fair skin was now glowing bright red.

"We are family by choice, but at the risk of sounding childish, I wanted us to be connected by blood and now we are."

We all approached Dreah and took turns enfolding her into a hug. We were a family by choice and not by blood, but we were a strong family unit despite that.

I loved the gift she had given us, as we were all connected by blood now. Even though it was only ceremonial, we were bonded for life and you just never knew when that connection might be necessary.

7

The family remained at the estate for a few more weeks to rest.

I was walking the grounds, trying to shake this creepy-crawly sensation that had me on edge, when Cipriano reached out, through our mental connection, to let me know that visitors were coming to the estate.

Two men, representing separate European dragon clans, had requested to speak with Cipriano about joining our place in the Ozarks. Sanctuary had been steadily growing over the past couple of years, as word spread of its existence.

There was an air of expectation that hung over the estate, like ominous clouds before a storm—a deluge just waiting to unload.

The strangers had arrived.

A flash of distrust exploded through my connection with

Cipriano, but quickly disappeared, before he directed, *"Come to the great room and convince Dreah to stay in her room."*

I rolled my eyes. I'd try, but that girl had a mind of her own. She was stubborn to a fault and I loved it.

As I made my way to the great room, an electric current crawled over my skin and made the hair on my arms stand on end. A feeling of inevitability washed over me and I stopped.

I did *not* want to enter that room.

Thick emotions permeated through the door to douse me in their residue. There was a mixed bag of feelings; distrust from Cipriano and expectation from the strangers. The rest of the family were oddly silent and void of emotion—never a good sign.

I was blasted by these emotions when I entered the room. I didn't bother trying to decipher them all, as there were too many to separate.

I looked towards the strangers and then to Cipriano, who stood staring at the pair without expression. I walked towards Cipriano and stood by his side in a show of support and solidarity.

The silence was uncomfortable.

To break the tension, I began to introduce myself, since no one else was doing the honors.

"Now that we're all here..." Cipriano began, interrupting me before I could begin.

"*Now*...we're all here," Dreah interrupted, as she came barging through the door.

She walked over to stand next to me, grabbing my hand as she did so. Her ring began to warm where our fingers were joined together. She gripped my hand tighter just before she let it go and placed her hands at her sides.

Cipriano began anew, "Now that we are *all* here, what can we do for you?"

The two strangers looked at each other with uncertainty, clearly they hadn't decided who would speak first. They spoke in unison, stumbling over each other.

"My name is Sterling..."

"My name is DeChadik..."

They stopped. DeChadik turned red, while Sterling merely nodded.

"I suppose we should have decided on the speaking order ahead of time. Apologies, My Lord," DeChadik said in deference to Cipriano.

It was still strange to hear Cipriano addressed as such, yet not surprising. He was leader of men and that was evident in how he carried himself and his interactions with the various clan leaders and their clansmen.

They treated me with respect, but mostly with distant awe, especially after Cipriano introduced me as the last true Phoenix.

I was their legend—their prophecy come to life. I felt like a fraud.

"I've come from a small clan in northern Romania. We have suffered too many losses because of the drampires' pursuit of immortality. Our clan can no longer afford to stay insular. I have repeatedly begged and finally succeeded, in convincing the remaining clansmen to seek an alliance outside of ourselves. I'm here to inquire about joining your sanctuary," DeChadik said with passion and desperation.

"I'm encouraged to hear that you heard of us so far away," Cipriano replied.

"We have minimal contact with other clans, but a messenger came to tell us about a new sanctuary for dragons. The concept of protection in numbers is extremely enticing. We have no mated dragons and there haven't been any dragon births in centuries. We are truly a dying breed. I left immediately to investigate."

The love and distress DeChadik felt for his clan's precarious position was evident to see and feel. His demeanor was forthright and open. He wasn't afraid to show vulnerability or admit that he desperately needed help. Some clans hadn't been as accepting and yet, they had come to us nonetheless.

Collectively, we had to change the mindset of these centuries-old clans. It should be relatively easy, I thought, and almost laughed out loud at the enormity of that task.

"Thank you for allowing me into your home," Sterling said, "I've been searching for our clan leader and his mate for over a quarter of a century, with no luck. I heard you were in Scotland twenty-five years ago and traveled here, on the off-chance that you may have some information about them," he addressed Cipriano.

"No, I'd already relocated to the States by then," Cipriano answered, but then asked, "Have you been to Scotland?"

"Yes, but the Scots were less than helpful. No one remembered them or anything about their mission. More than likely, they simply refused to say," Sterling finished, clearly disgruntled.

"The Scots don't particularly like strangers. I swear, they have to be descended from dragons with how little they are willing to interact with others," Cipriano stated deadpan, then barked out a laugh, but just as quickly sobered.

Sterling wasn't happy, if the brooding stare he shot Cipriano was anything to go by. I noticed Sterling avoided looking at me, though he did scan the others, if only briefly. He kept his attention focused on Cipriano the entire time, while DeChadik smiled at me and the others. I sensed he was curious about who I might be.

"My name is Charani," I interjected since no one else was going to introduce me, "I'm pleased to meet you, DeChadik and Sterling. As you know, this is Cipriano, my brother, and next to me is my sister, Dreah."

This pulled Sterling's attention briefly in our direction.

"By the window are my brothers, Tarrin and Tauric. And over by the fireplace is my brother, Ian, and his mate and my sister, Isabella."

"I am pleased to meet all of you. I can't wait to relocate my small clan to sanctuary. I feel we can thrive and flourish there," ingratiated DeChadik.

Sterling tipped his head.

DeChadik and Sterling were both tall, as was typical of male dragons, but that was where the similarities ended. Sterling was dark and brooding and DeChadik was all light and sunshine, except for his brown, earthy-colored eyes.

Sterling radiated authority, much like Cipriano did. They were definitely contemporaries. Whereas, DeChadik lacked the command of the other males in the room, but he seemed a likable sort and would blend in well at sanctuary. He might be good at bringing the clans together with his easy going nature.

I continued to watch Sterling and DeChadik as they interacted with the family. DeChadik's aura was swirling with the blue of our dragon, as well as a subtle pink and green iridescence. However, Sterling's aura was much more contained and I only saw our dragon blue.

Sterling continued to explain how he and his clansmen had tried to piece together what happened to their leader and his mate while on their mission to Scotland.

"We'd been dealing with an increase in brethren deaths and wanted to form a task force with other dragon clans to stop drampires from killing our people. Our clan is small and we've suffered grievously."

The sensation of inevitability increased exponentially. This moment, this interaction felt like it would become a defining moment in my life. Sterling's gaze swung towards me and momentarily lingered on my face. He focused on my eyes before he turned back to Cipriano. The intensity of his emotions receded, as if behind a shield of protection, similar to what I did. I couldn't tell what exactly he was feeling, just that some strong emotion had moved him.

He addressed Cipriano, "I was told that you and your clan originated from Scotland. Do you perhaps still have clansmen there that might be of assistance?"

I could feel Cipriano's demeanor marginally relax as Sterling spoke with him about his clan's plight. Their clans had suffered similarly and at the hands of a common enemy. They would be united in that, just as we hoped all the clans coming to sanctuary would be.

"No, I'm sorry to say. I don't have clansmen there that can help you. Do you think they are still alive somewhere?"

I opened myself up to the collective and to Sterling and nearly fell over from the brief influx of emotions.

"You know what happened to them, don't you?" I asked.

Reluctantly he turned his head towards me, causing his long dark hair to sway and partially obscure his face. But once it settled, I had a clear view of the pain swirling in his crystal blue eyes. It caused my heart to pinch in sympathy at his loss. I knew what was coming—could feel it.

"We know they're gone," Sterling said, "I felt it resonate through my dragon essence the moment they each died."

8

The rest of that day and the next morning, were spent making plans for DeChadik's clansmen to relocate to the Ozarks. We had streamlined the process at this point, so it wasn't too difficult. Plus, his clan was small and we had enough homes to immediately accommodate them.

DeChadik would be leaving in the morning, so we decided to have a special dinner tonight. Isabella and I were driving downtown to pick up dinner, while Cipriano and Ian finalized the relocation plans with DeChadik.

Sterling was tagging along. I think he wanted to escape DeChadik. He was going to be bored senseless, but it would serve him right for inviting himself on our little outing.

I knew there was more to Sterling than just as an emissary seeking information—his emotions were too locked-down behind an impenetrable mask. I did feel his emotions briefly, but this inability to *feel* him gave me pause. I'd always been able to sense and feel other people's emotions and the fact that I couldn't...

He would be watched and our trust withheld until we could ascertain his motives.

THE ECHO of raised voices slammed into us as soon as we stepped out the front door. Alarmed by the potential threat, I felt a familiar static electricity—the precursor to shifting. I quickly reached out to stop Sterling, knowing he was the source.

"It's okay, Sterling. It's merely Dreah having her defense lessons with the twins."

The twins were fanatical about her having the ability to protect herself and I agreed with them. She'd been having lessons in self-protection for years now. It didn't hurt that Dreah adored the twins and wanted to learn everything she could, especially after all that she'd suffered at the hands of Hulbetto.

We made our way over to the west lawn, careful not to interrupt or distract Dreah as the twins sparred with her. We sat quietly on the edge of the fountain Cipriano had commissioned years ago by a local metal artisan.

It featured a magnificent copper dragon caught in mid-flight. It was old and weathered with a beautiful patina to its scales. I loved to sit here in peaceful contemplation.

After long walks around the estate and through the rose garden, Dreah and I would come here to talk, as would Isabella and I. The tinkling water was soothing to my ears and my soul.

Tarrin and Tauric were a rare set of identical twins. With their white-blonde hair and Nordic blue eyes, they could have passed for Viking warriors. They were quiet, but gentle giants —unless you tried to hurt their family. I wouldn't want to be on the receiving end of their battle skills when they were in human-form or when they were flying in their fierce dragon-form.

No drampire would dare to come after them as Death would be the result.

Dreah was a beautiful contrast to the twins coloring with her auburn hair and amber eyes. She was diminutive in height and had a slight frame, but she used those to her advantage as she was extremely agile and deceptively strong.

She was poetry in motion, but despite being adept with today's weapon of choice, the staff, Tarrin was pushing her hard. They wanted her to be fearsome and she was. I loved sparring with her and Isabella. The three of us often had lessons together.

Tauric snuck in behind Dreah to take her unawares, while Tarrin was engaging her from the front.

She whirled around with a grunt to raise her staff, blocking his attack. The wooden staffs connected hard—the sound resonating across the lawn.

Dreah whipped back around, expecting Tarrin's attack—which came straight away and with no break in the action. He swept his staff at her feet. Jumping over it, Dreah kicked out with her foot and caught him in the abdomen—knocking the breath from his lungs.

In the process of landing, Tauric managed to wrest the staff from her hand. She jumped out of the way, when he jabbed it forward for a kidney blow.

Dreah murmured a few words under her breath and waved her hand, then snapped her fingers. A new staff appeared, as if out of thin air, into her opened and awaiting hand—she immediately dropped into a fighting stance and raised her chin.

The twins laughed at her cocky challenge.

"We concede this round, *lille venn*," Tauric told Dreah, calling her little one, as we all liked to do.

The three of them bowed to each other and then to their audience. Dreah blushed when she realized Sterling was with us and had seen her show of magic. She looked directly at me and shrugged her shoulders.

"Dreah you have far exceeded me in skill," I praised.

"No way, Charani. You're my hero, along with Isabella!"

"Thank you, sweet Dreah." Isabella said, then asked, "We are heading downtown to pick up dinner. Did you want to tag along with us?"

"Thank you, but I have a few things to do. I'll see you guys at dinner, okay?" she replied, and then headed off towards the house after saying goodbye to everyone, including Sterling.

As we headed downtown, Isabella intentionally drove by some of Kansas City's historical buildings and monuments. I described the history as I knew it, and Sterling avidly listened, seemingly interested in our city's culture.

As we passed Liberty Memorial Tower, where the only National World War I Museum and Memorial was located, I explained to Sterling how it was the only museum in America dedicated to sharing the stories of the Great War.

Liberty Memorial was an inspirational piece of art and history that sat atop a hill overlooking all of Kansas City. Below it and towards the north was Union Station.

The architecture of Union Station was both beautiful and intricate. The old train station had been lovingly restored and repurposed hosting a variety of exhibits throughout the year.

AT DINNER THAT EVENING, we chatted about our trip downtown and about both of their clans. DeChadik spoke eloquently about his life in Romania and about his clansmen. He was excited about the upcoming move and it was evident that he couldn't wait to leave tomorrow.

"I'll leave straight away. The sooner I get my clansmen to sanctuary, the better I'll feel and can relax knowing they are safe and will be cared for."

Sterling was more reserved. He would answer direct questions, but didn't volunteer information as readily as DeChadik. Their personalities were completely opposite of each other.

"Sterling, how did you and DeChadik come to travel together?" Ian asked from across the table.

I was so glad he asked that question, as I couldn't picture them hanging out and being friends. Not at all!

Unsurprisingly, DeChadik answered. "When the messenger left Romania, I left with him to start the process as soon as possible. He told me that he knew of a clan without a leader and felt they were in dire need of help. He said we would stop there first and then travel to the States."

We all waited to see how Sterling would respond to that not so veiled insult. But he was an utter disappointment, I thought while smiling.

Sterling had looked up from his plate, fork arrested mid-air, to gaze in DeChadik's direction. His face devoid of expression or emotion. His lack of response was not all surprising.

"Interesting that this messenger would know all about Sterling's clan. I have no doubt that he's a very capable leader, " Isabella said in Sterling's defense, when he would offer none for himself.

Dinner continued and afterwards we all went our separate ways. DeChadik thanked Cipriano and the family for our hospitality and stated that he would be leaving tonight after resting for a bit. He decided to take advantage of the darkness to travel home tonight, instead of waiting until tomorrow.

Ian and Isabella wished him well then left, hand-in-hand, for their nightly walk through the gardens and around the estate. Isabella had an affinity for plants and the flora and fauna thrived under her doting. She treated the flowers as if they were her, be-leafed and delicately petaled, babies.

Ian helped her with the gardens when we were at the estate in Kansas City—we all did. There was something quite soothing about working with the soil and coaxing the budding plants to life and into full bloom.

The hothouse was one of my favorite places to be. The heady, exotic perfume of the flowers, especially the roses, lilacs, the mock orange trees, gradually supplanted the noxious stench from the asylum dungeon. It clung tenaciously to my olfactory memories haunting me with the horrid memories of my confinement.

Dreah decided to go to her room to watch TV, but I suspected she might watch videos of her parents. We had rescued them from her house before they were lost or taken and destroyed by someone.

The pain of seeing and hearing her parents was excruciating. I knew it was, because I sat with Dreah every time she watched those videos, reminiscing, then held her body, as she shook with the force of her grief in the aftermath. At times, I worried she'd shake herself into a million shards of sadness.

To love and be loved like that was unfathomable for me, but I was learning.

She refused to forget them—what they looked like or the intonation of their voices. Her strength and determination were impressive, as was her warrior heart.

Thankfully, time had dulled grief's edge and she could appreciate the memories without having to drown in despair.

The love I had for Dreah and my chosen family was fierce and unconditional. I would die for them—without hesitation.

Cipriano and the twins went to the great room with Sterling. I wasn't tired, but didn't feel much like socializing, so I decided to go to the music room.

I should have gone to bed.

9

Why do I feel the need to torture myself? My demons do it on a regular basis within the dreaming—that should have been enough, but no, evidently I had to join in with a little self-inflicted pain.

I really should have gone to bed, but I didn't.

As I made my way to the music room, I happened to see Ian and Isabella through the french doors. They were walking through the garden enjoying some alone time, which is why we'd returned to the estate in the first place. We had finally taken some time away from sanctuary and the business of getting the incoming clans settled into their new homes.

Sterling and DeChadik had interrupted our respite, but it was our mission to unite the clans, so these interruptions were to be expected. Eventually, we would learn how to balance the constant demands for our time with caring for ourselves amidst the chaos.

Tonight, I was hoping the music room would be that oasis of peace for me.

I loved playing the cello, but did so for pleasure now and not so much for creating my musical protection. Cipriano was right in that, it really was a mental exercise to create a shield, though initially it had helped me to visualize what I needed to do.

The first notes of protection I'd ever created were in my dungeon hell at the asylum. I hadn't known what I was doing, I'd only wanted to shut out the screaming voices of the lost, as I liked to call them—they'd been inconsolable at the time. Later, I would dub them 'the collective', my people, my brethren, and they were all dragons.

I'd always loved playing music, especially the piano. So creating music had been a natural way to temper the pain from the voices ripping at my mind.

As I waited to die—those golden notes had floated around me in the oppressive darkness—shocking me with their appearance. At the time, I'd thought those shimmering, translucent notes were a figment of my imagination, a hallucination of my dying mind. But those beautiful musical notes had been the first iteration of my musical shield—a rudimentary attempt, in comparison to the shield I utilized now.

I'd played with various ways to protect myself, including stacking bricks within my mind, but that had felt mentally laborious to use and reminded me too much of dying in the dark suffocation of the dungeon basement at the asylum.

However, I adamantly refused to use the piano as a way to learn as there were too many horrible memories associated with it from my past and chose to use the cello instead.

Technically, I didn't have to physically play the cello to weave the notes for my shield, but it helped. Besides, the cello had become my solace and my voice—the notes weeping when I could not.

When I entered the music room tonight, I did something I hadn't done since I was a child of eight years old—I sat down at the piano.

My shaking, indecisive fingers hovered over the avoided, but not forgotten, piano keys, as my heart and mind warred for supremacy. I finally gave into the compulsion and set my fingers lightly upon the black and whites of the Bösendorfer Imperial Grand.

The keys felt foreign and yet, familiar under my questing fingers. They caressed a melancholic tune from the piano, a reflection of the emotions I stuffed behind my, "I have it all together," façade. Like the cello, the piano was a weeping reflection of my soul.

Something was pulling these emotions forward today, perhaps the sorrow of Sterling's story. I didn't know, so I quit trying to analyze what I was feeling and gave in to the emotions. The golden notes floated through the air around me, sad and beautiful all at once.

"You play beautifully, Charani, but my heart fare weeps with the sadness of your music."

My fingers hit the keys with a hard, discordant sound, "DeChadik, I didn't hear you come in." I said, perturbed at the interruption.

I'd been so lost in the music that I hadn't heard his approach. How long had he stood there listening before making his comment? I would have rather experienced this monumental moment in peace and privacy.

"I apologize for interrupting. I'll leave you to your music," DeChadik said, before turning to leave.

"Wait. I do apologize. I haven't played the piano for some years and it…"

"Think nothing of it," he said, stopping before the french doors that opened out to the west gardens, "I should rest, in any case. I was at loose ends, tired and yet excited for the next stage of my life…for my clan's life. I'll bid you goodnight and let you get back to making those keys cry."

Looking out to where his gaze had been captured, I saw Ian and Isabella walking hand-in-hand. Not realizing he had an audience, Ian suddenly pulled Isabella into his arms and kissed her with a passion I didn't understand and had never experienced.

My heart felt dead in that regard because despite the numerous clansmen I'd met over the past few years, not one had stirred my heart. If a mate existed for me, I had yet to meet him. I feared he may have already been killed by the drampires to supply their thirst for immortality.

That would be more to my luck. I had mixed feelings

about mates and their commitment to each other. How does one surrender all that they are; and, know that if they died, their mate would die, too? I didn't think that level of connection was for me.

DeChadik avidly watched their passionate moment, staring intently at the mated pair. They made beautiful mates and were so cute together, often finishing each other sentences. They had been mated for some time now.

Ian was a Phoenix Dragon, like Cipriano and I. He had a black stripe through his auburn hair, whereas Cipriano's dark hair had a white stripe and my long black hair had a red stripe. We were each different, though still shared the dragon essence similarities.

Isabella had the purest soul and was just as beautiful on the outside as she was on the inside. She was fiercely devoted to her family and would kill anyone that dared to hurt them. But she had a sweet temperament that matched her delicate features. She reminded me of Violet—her beauty was ethereal.

Isabella had long chestnut hair and unusual eyes. They were a beautiful blend of sage green and amber—with the amber radiating from their center, like a star. I'd never seen eyes like hers before and just loved their uniqueness. She told me it was a defect called 'central heterochromia.' I didn't see it as a defect and luckily she didn't either.

Ian suddenly dropped to his knees before Isabella and placed his cheek against her abdomen—wrapping his arms around her hips. Then cupped her abdomen and placed a kiss there, as if for their unborn child growing safe within.

I barely contained my gasp, but DeChadik wasn't able to censor his and let it fly. The impact of what this could mean for them, for us and for the dragon culture as a whole was enormous.

Besides me, their child would be the first dragon to have been born in centuries. Their child would be the next generation and the dragons' new hope. I would protect their child with my very life—we all would.

DeChadik nodded and said goodnight and I was left alone with my mixed feelings for company.

Later that night, I was awakened by the sound of Dreah crying out in her sleep. I pulled on my robe and hurried down the hallway to her room. Sterling met me at her door. I looked at him questioningly and he merely raised his eyebrow.

We walked into the room together. Dreah was sitting up in her bed crying—lost in whatever vision held her captive.

10

I scowled at him. I wanted to protect Dreah. I didn't want anyone to know she experienced these prophetic visions, especially, Sterling and DeChadik, wherever he was, two strangers in our household. The fewer people that knew, the better it would be for Dreah.

I hurried to her side and sat on the bed next to her and picked up her hand. I held her ring next to my skin and knew from experience that it would be warm to the touch. The ring was my gateway to Dreah's mind...

Hulbetto was wielding Aiden, the Sword of Dramascus, against a man with dark hair and blue eyes. The man was in a fight for his life. Though bleeding from multiple wounds, he refused to bow down under Hulbetto and his sword.

I watched as he attempted to shift, but couldn't. He was mortally wounded and they both knew.

This was a vision from the past because I had killed Hulbetto a few years ago, but despite that, I could feel the emotions coming from the man. There was a sense of inevitability. He was angry and sad, full of regret and of love. He was worried for his mate and her safety.

I could feel all of his emotions, as if they were my own. His desire to kill Hulbetto and his determination to return to his mate were palpable. My heart ached for what I realized would occur.

His attention was focused solely on Hulbetto, so he didn't realize the apprentice had snuck up behind him. I wanted to call out a warning to him, but caught myself before the words could be vocalized. I looked at Dreah, empathizing for what she must likewise be feeling as we watched the defenseless man fight to live.

The apprentice drew back his bowstring, notched his arrow of Damascus steel and unleashed it to find a home straight through the man's back and out through his heart. Shock and pain etched his face, but remorse and longing were evident in his voice as he cried out with his impotent fury.

Before he closed his eyes and died among the standing stones, he managed a final whispered, "I love you, Júlia. Stay strong, my beloved."

The scene flashed to a beautiful woman with blonde hair and bright green eyes—wide with shock and shimmering with tears. She reached out her hand, as if to touch her mate one last time before he disappeared, though she knew she'd follow him shortly.

I was pulled from the vision when I felt a hand rest upon my shoulder. I didn't have to open my eyes to know it was Cipriano. I saw that Sterling was at the end of the bed in a watchful, yet guarding stance. A lone sentinel, he watched over Dreah and I, scanning our faces—for what, I wasn't sure.

When Dreah emerged from her vision, Sterling walked closer and knelt down beside her. The twins came in and scowled at Sterling for daring to be near her.

"Are you all right, little one," he asked gently.

Dreah turned to Sterling, assessing him with her gaze. To give him credit, he let her look her fill without so much as a blink of his blue eyes. She nodded in response to his question and then turned to address the room.

"May I please speak with Sterling and Charani alone?" Dreah asked.

Though reluctant to leave, everyone complied. Once the three of us were alone and the door was shut, she explained to Sterling what she'd seen within her mind—mirroring what I'd seen as well.

"I saw the ancient drampire, Hulbetto, kill a male dragon with the Sword of Dramascus," she told Sterling.

"I wondered whether the sword was real or a myth. We've all heard rumors, but no one I know has ever seen it, or rather lived to say that they had. I'm sorry you had to witness such brutality," Sterling told to Dreah.

"I've seen his brutality first hand and felt it, as he carved into my skin," she said, showing him her scars. "Hulbetto killed my parents and stole their dragon essence," she told him simply.

The scars marring her skin were nearly gone now, but they were the indelible reminders from her time with Hulbetto. It was the *invisible* ones that refused to fade or to heal. They continued to bleed with her pain and her grief at the loss of her parents.

Dreah continued, "The man was mortally wounded, but fought to live. He fought to reach his beloved mate."

"We mate for life and are eternally bonded, so any dragon would have fought until his last breath was stolen from him. His mate would have died, too, I'm sorry to say. It's the way of the dragon."

"Yes," I said, agreeing with Sterling.

Cipriano and the others had taught Dreah and I all about dragon culture and lore.

"Before I was pulled from the vision, I saw his mate. Her eyes were wide with shock and filled with unshed tears, and..

With her imminent death," I finished.

Dreah turned to look at me with a compassion I didn't pretend to understand. She held out her hand for me to hold and reached for Sterling's. She placed our hands, so that her hand and the ring, were sandwiched between ours. She clearly wanted us both touching her ring.

She opened her mind to the vision again and gave Sterling a taste of what she'd seen.

His eyes were closed as the vision opened. Once again I saw Hulbetto wielding Aiden and the dark-haired man covered in injuries. Sterling gasped and his eyes flew open.

He looked at Dreah and at me. Pain etched on his face, as if he, too, had felt the man's pain.

The vision continued but picked up where it had left off for me, when Cipriano had touched my shoulder. The dark-haired man had died and his beautiful mate had felt his death tear through her soul, knowing she was next, or so I thought...

She reached out her hand, as if to touch her mate one last time before he disappeared, though she knew she'd soon follow. With her other hand, she gently cradled her abdomen where their beloved, yet unexpected child rested quietly under her heart.

It was my turn to gasp. My heart ached for their child.

That child lost its father before it was ever born and then its mother shortly thereafter—basically delivered into this world an orphan—courtesy of Hulbetto.

I understood that pain and so did Dreah, as we were both orphans. Her parents had been killed by Hulbetto and mine had given me away.

The vision ended, but we remained silent in its aftermath.

Sterling looked at Dreah and then turned to me, shock evident on his face, his emotions evident in his broken whisper, "I didn't know she was with child."

11

"Did you know this woman, Sterling? This man?" I asked.

"I did," he said. "They were the leaders of our clan."

"Her name was Júlia and her mate was Kristóf. Despite being mated, they chose to stay with their clan, rather than go into hiding. They wanted to be an example of strength and determination. We are a strong race, but somehow the drampires still managed to hunt us down, reap our dragons of their essence, and kill our brethren."

"Charani? Sterling?" Dreah interjected, "There's more," she said, holding out her hand.

I placed my hand over hers and Sterling placed his under and we waited for the next vision to start. I grabbed her other hand and braced myself for what would unfold within the landscape of Dreah's mind...

The vision showed Júlia in a hospital and laboring. The nurses were asking her questions about having any family nearby. She replied that she was recently widowed. I could feel the empathy from the nurses who were by her side. The joyous moment was weighted in sorrow and they all felt it.

Tears of pain and grief glistened on Júlia's pale cheeks and caught strands of her blonde hair. One of the nurses, Caitlyn I heard her called, turned away to wipe her eyes, clearly touched by the young woman's grief and wanting to hide it from the others.

"Come on now, lovey," Caitlyn said to Júlia, "You've got ta push your wee one oot."

The nurses helped to deliver Júlia and Kristóf's child—a baby girl. Once washed and swaddled, they handed her over to Júlia. The love she had for her daughter filled the room and the nurses glowed with the abundance, though Júlia remained pale.

She knew what was coming and there was nothing she could do to stop it. The inevitable end was near. Her death.

She held her daughter cradled in her arms and nestled right next to her heart—constantly touching her and stroking her pink cheeks. She kissed each of her fingers and counted all ten of her toes.

It was beautiful to see and heartbreaking to watch. Tears slid down my cheeks at the poignant moment and for once, I didn't suppress the overwhelming emotions. I looked over to Sterling, who was likewise affected, though his eyes were closed concentrating on the scene, tears flowed unchecked in a river of sorrow.

I didn't need to look at Dreah to feel her sorrow. We were all captured within this heart-wrenching scene, knowing without a doubt, how it would all end, yet helpless to change the outcome...

"Our beloved child, we have wanted you for so long. We never thought to conceive, though we prayed for you every day. Your father loved you so much, little one. Oh, he would have loved to see you in person—to hold you close to his heart. I know he can see you from the other side and feel how strong you are.

"I can't bear to leave you...but I know...I know that I will and soon," Júlia told her daughter.

Her emotions caused her breath to hitch, just as they did mine. Not wanting to intrude, Violet sent gentle waves of warmth from where she lay inked on my skin, it was her way of sending comfort as I watched the mother and daughter...

"Be happy, my daughter. One of the nurses will adopt you, the seed has already been planted. You will be well loved, I know it. She's longed for a child, but was not blessed with one of her own, so I will give her my most treasured gift— you. She has a beautiful aura that glows with love and a healing spirit."

Her daughter was starting to cry and fuss, sensing her mother's distress.

"Be strong, beautiful."

Caitlyn came over to ask Júlia if she was feeling okay. Júlia shook her head, without answering, but the answer was clear. She was rapidly losing color. She placed her daughter to her breast.

"Before I go, baby girl...you...you must drink of my essence as you drink from my breast. I will give you all that I am and...as I do...I will tell you about your name.

"We chose your name deliberately for its meaning— beloved child. That is what you are to us. I wish I could be here to remind you just how cherished you are, but you will have my essence running through your soul. I will give you every ounce as I fade...that way, I will...I will always be within you."

She whispered furtively to her daughter of her love and of her regret. She knew her time had come. I could see the vibrance of her aura diminishing as she began the transition to the other side to join her mate, Kristóf...

"Drink of my essence. Take in all that I am, so that you may live eternally and fulfill your destiny. Remember that we loved you...fiercely and without reserve."

"I love you...Mia."

I quickly wove the strongest musical shield I'd ever created. I couldn't allow Sterling to know what that name meant to me.

Oh God!

Dreah knew and understood. I could hardly catch my breath for the tears that threatened to choke me as they poured down my throat. But the pain wasn't over yet.

1 2

I watched helplessly as Júlia, my beautiful mother, transferred every bit of her dragon essence to me before she faded to the other side. I didn't even know that was possible...

The nurses took me from her arms so they could attempt to save her life, but it was futile. She was dragon, they just didn't know that. The infant that I'd been was crying inconsolably and so was I, though only the infant-me could give free reign to the devastating emotions—empathic, even then.

Caitlyn held me in her arms offering comfort, words of love, and stability with the future she had planned out. Caitlyn doted upon the infant me waiting for the day that she could adopt me. The hospital dictated a waiting period of six months to allow for family to come forward. I was placed in an orphanage of sorts that was attached to the hospital.

Everything was going as planned, until Dr. Hanley saw me on his walk through the hospital as a visiting physician. He felt the current of my true self and manipulated the normals into getting what he wanted—me!

Hanley and Hulbetto were responsible for destroying what should have been my life. They killed my parents and took me from the woman my mother chose to raise me.

They gave me to Sebastian and Helena, who ultimately hated me for what I became—imperfect. They threw me away when I was eight years-old, and incarcerated in Hanley's asylum for not being their perfect little Snow White.

Hanley carved into my skin, then stole and imprisoned a portion of my essence in Hulbetto's Amulet of the Dead and allowed me to die from malicious neglect!

My shield was fortified and impenetrable by everyone except Violet, as she was still resting against my skin. I would have blocked her if I could, or asked her to shift, but she couldn't right now, not in front of Dreah and Sterling.

I let go of Dreah's hand when the vision ended, just as Helena was carrying me away from the hospital. In the background, I could feel the confusion and sadness from Caitlyn, another victim to the drampires diabolic machinations.

I didn't know how to deal with the revelation that I had been loved. I had been valued. I had been wanted. As a result, I didn't dare move or speak, I was far too raw and yet, I was consumed by hate and rage.

"I need to find the people who took baby Mia from that hospital in Scotland. I sensed Hulbetto was involved and the doctor, too," Sterling commented, "but she could be anywhere."

Dreah answered him, because words were beyond me, and, with my shield up, I had no idea the state of his emotions. He was difficult to read even when I was wide open, but the tenor of his words conveyed his agitation.

"Dr. Hanley was his apprentice. They are both dead now. We don't know who that couple was or where they could be with Mia. If I have another vision, I will let you know," Dreah told him, and then turned to look at me, adding, "both of you."

"I have to find her. It's imperative," Sterling said, shoving his hand through his dark hair.

"Why..." I tried to ask, but croaked instead. I cleared my throat several times to get my husky voice working again.

"Why is it imperative, Sterling? Perhaps Mia is happy in her new home," I replied, my voice huskier than normal, as I barely hid my emotions from coloring my words.

"I realize she is an adult now and doesn't need parents to raise her. But as the daughter of our leaders, the clan leadership would fall to her and her sibling."

I had avoided looking at Sterling until that moment, "Mia has a sibling?"

"Yes, she does," he said, then paused. in reflection and debate.

I understood all too well the need to protect coveted information such as this. I was doing the same. But, I wanted to know who this sibling was and where they were, more than he could possibly understand.

"Together, Mia and her sibling would share responsibility for the leadership of their parents' clan. Her brother has been doing it alone while the clan searched for answers to where Kristóf and Júlia were located. We knew they had moved on to the other side, but not how. I'd hoped there might be a child, given the delay I felt between the death of Kristóf and Júlia."

"Isn't it unusual that you felt their deaths so acutely?" I asked.

"As a child, Júlia saved my life with the healing of her dragon essence. In that moment, she became a mother to me and I loved her as a son would love his mother. She was such a selfless soul and transformed my father's life when they mated."

I couldn't contain the gasp that escaped my mouth. I had a brother and his name was Sterling.

"I have to go," I said desperately.

Leaning forward, I kissed Dreah gently on the forehead and told her to get some rest.

"Reach out to Cipriano, would you? Let him know that you're okay and that I had to run an errand."

"I will, Charani, but you do realize it's the middle of the night, don't you? Can you go in the morning?"

"No, I have to go now."

I nodded to Sterling to follow me out of Dreah's room. As we left, I heard Dreah call out, "I love you, Charani. Be well."

She was the daughter of my heart. I understood exactly what Sterling was saying in regards to his bond with Júlia. I had the same with Dreah.

"I'll chat with you tomorrow," I said abruptly.

I turned and ran down the stairs and out the front door, still wearing my robe. By allowing my emotions to overrule my head, I completely ignored one of the most sacred tenets of safety and self-preservation, be cognizant of your surroundings.

As soon as I cleared the front door, I rapidly shifted to shadow and just as quickly, shifted into my dragon. I fled the estate, like the hounds of hell were chasing me.

I had no destination chosen, just away from the demons clawing at my mind. Running proved futile, just as I knew it would. I couldn't escape my mind nor the implications screaming at me.

Sterling was my brother!

How do I reset my way of thinking? How would I adjust to this new reality versus the reality I'd come to believe? Everything I knew about myself—who I was and where I'd come from—had been false. As a result, I could feel the stability of my foundation crumbling beneath me.

I kept flying away. That's all I wanted—to be away from everyone and everything.

There were numerous caves around the estate and

throughout Missouri, so I headed for one that I frequented all too often. It was hidden away from normals, but accessible to me, which made it the perfect hideaway.

When my demons became too vocal to contain, I'd escape here to be alone. I wouldn't allow my problems to stress the family, besides I preferred to fight my demons alone. Once I beat the voices back into temporary submission, only then would I allow myself to return to the estate.

My demons and I had a love-hate relationship.

They loved to torment me and I hated the hold they had over my mind and my emotions. They loved to attack me when I was asleep and in the dreaming. They would remind me and quite vocally, how I was worthless and then illustrate that fact with vignettes I had to relive from my time in the asylum dungeon.

Good times!

Once I arrived at the cave, I shifted seamlessly from dragon to human and sat on a rock that flanked the secluded entrance to my cave. The estate was located miles away to the west. I'd created a home there—a surrogate family. What would this new information mean for them? For us?

The vision of my father, Kristóf, fighting for his life against Hulbetto and with the same apprentice who had tried to kill me, kept playing through my mind.

He'd tried to shift repeatedly, but his injuries had made the transition impossible. He was denied the well of his dragon essence where all the magic originated.

Most dragons lived for a very long time, centuries even, and some were immortal, like Phoenix Dragons. A mortally injured dragon could not survive without intervention, even if they were immortal. Kristóf might have survived if a dragon with healing abilities had been nearby.

However, no dragon could survive an arrow shot through the heart, especially one made with Damascus steel. There would be no coming back from that, no matter what.

It wasn't fair that we had this weakness. What was the drampires' weakness, besides their mortality, which they'd managed to circumvent? There had to be something and I would find it.

I vowed here and now, that I would find Hulbetto's apprentice and kill him. He would pay for all the grief and pain he had caused me and my family. Not only was he responsible for killing my father and therefore, my mother, he had stolen Aiden, still trapped within the Sword of Dramascus, when he ran from the warehouse.

Hulbetto was dead. Dr. Hanley was dead. The apprentice would be next.

Death, pain, loss, grief, and rage threatened to tear me apart. Visions of my birth and my mother's death left me emotionally defenseless. I'd just lost both of my parents today and the weight of that grief was suffocating.

I couldn't help but feel responsible for my mother's death or at least for the fact that her joining my father on the other side, had been delayed. I couldn't imagine how she must have felt knowing that her death was inevitable and there was no way for it to be averted.

Was she in a constant state of emotional warfare? Anticipation and dread fighting for supremacy within her heart? Was she anticipating the moment she would transition to the other side to be with her mate, my father? Was she dreading the moment she would deliver her daughter and take her last breath, leaving her daughter defenseless?

No matter how I tried to analyze what I'd seen or how I tried to put a positive spin on it—I couldn't. Nothing good had come from what I'd learned.

I gained a brother, that was a positive, I think.

Kristóf and Júlia's love had been tangible within Dreah's vision and it continued to echo through me—enveloping me with its resonance. Sebastian and Helena had been connected in a similar way and despite being normals, they behaved as if they were mated dragons.

Thinking about my adoptive parents elicited mixed feelings. I saw the love that Helena had for me in Dreah's vision when Hanley handed me over to her. I'd heard the story of my adoption hundreds of times, but watching it within Dreah's vision gave the moment added depth and perspective.

My cheeks and lips really had been chapped red, just like she'd always told me. My black hair was wild and standing straight up and my blue eyes were wide with fear, but when I saw Helena, I'd practically jumped into her arms...

"We shall name you, Sarah. It means princess and you, my

darling, will be ours, and with your blue eyes and black hair, you'll be our little Snow White."

I would be many things in my life, but I'd never be a princess and I was only their Snow White until that fateful night. That's when everything changed and the world as I knew it had ceased to exist.

I've tried to capture the remnants of that love, but it was overshadowed by their shame. I wondered where they were now and how they were. They believed I died in a fire at the asylum.

Would the lens of time grant them a different perspective of me? Would they ever remember me with fondness, if not with love?

"I'm sure they loved you, My Lady. Perhaps they love you still and mourn your death," Violet said, as she shifted off my skin to sit upon my knee.

She didn't look at me, but looked out over the view. We had been together long enough, that she knew exactly what I needed and when. No one knew of her existence except Cipriano, who had been there the day I'd found her. She wanted privacy, which I completely understood and therefore, respected her wishes.

Her long tricolored hair was hanging down her back and between her beautiful wings. Shifting had caused random strands of her hair to become tangled with her wings, so she flapped them with an impatient huff when the strands didn't settle perfectly into place.

Though laughing at her pique, I reached forward to straighten the wayward locks of her hair.

"You're a mess, Violet!"

She looked over her shoulder at me, her purple eyes conveying her thoughts to perfection. I shook my head and laughed.

Pot and kettle.

"My Lady?"

"Yes?"

"I think it wonderful that you now have a brother. A real brother, Charani. You've chosen each member of your surrogate family, of which I'm a part of—thank you very much," she said with a nod of her head. "There are several brothers in that family now, but Sterling has no family, only you, and he doesn't even know that yet."

Violet had a way of breaking things down to the simplest of terms.

"You're right, but before I address the issue of my brother, I think I'll mourn Kristóf and Júlia in private for a little while longer. It'll be our secret for now," I told her.

I had come to love and appreciate my little faery. Violet had become a close friend to me, like Isabella and Dreah. They were the sisters of my heart.

Violet rarely shifted off my skin, preferring to rest there. When I asked her why, the answer she gave was just vague enough to be a non-answer, which was okay. I didn't need to understand, as long as she was happy.

Her demons rode her hard, just as mine did. We both carried internal scars that continued to affect how we interacted with the world around us, like Violet hiding as vibrant ink upon my skin, instead of moving on.

The past would always and forever impact the future. The question was whether Violet and I would allow that past to blind us to the present and deny us our future. Would we always remain a slave to our demons?

1 4

We returned to the estate because I felt terrible for leaving Dreah alone to deal with the vision of my parents' death and my birth. Hell, I could hardly process it and I was older than she was. I flew back the same way I'd left, though not as haphazardly and not as if the hounds of hell were chasing me.

When I was near the estate, I decided to go sit on the edge of the dragon fountain that Dreah and I loved so much. As I shifted on the lawn near the fountain, I saw that Dreah had the same idea.

"You're pretty smart," I said.

The moonlight cast shadows across the yard, but illuminated her pale skin until it was glowing with a soft luminescence. She gave me a knowing smile, as I sat down next to her.

"I'm sorry I left so abruptly, sis. It's inexcusable that you had to deal with the aftermath of your vision by yourself."

"Charani, stop. I know you still think of me as a little girl and in some ways, I still am. But I'm not and haven't been for a long while. Life forced me to mature. It is what it is, and I can't do anything about it. That vision was difficult to see and feel, but…"

"I know and I'm so sorry," I interrupted her, "for leaving you. It was unconscionable."

I felt terrible. We had a close relationship, like two sisters or a mother and daughter. When she looked younger, it was more of the mother-daughter type relationship. But now that she was an adult, we had transitioned to more of a sister relationship. Either way, we loved one another fiercely and without reserve.

Dreah sighed, sounding exasperated, then said, "You didn't let me finish. That vision was difficult to see and to feel, without a doubt. But it was excruciating to know what that vision meant to you. I'm so sorry that you had to watch your parents die. I know exactly what that pain feels like and how deep it cuts. I would have spared you its bite, if I could have."

She reached out to hold my hand, offering comfort.

"It's a relief to know that I wasn't given away and discarded like trash—unloved and unwanted. Kristóf and Júlia had loved and wanted their child yet, neither one of them would get to watch her grow and mature."

"Watch *you* grow, Charani. That baby was *you*, Mia!"

I couldn't speak, so I nodded to concede her point. Mia

was what I had named one of the voices inside my head, the others had mostly belonged to the collective.

"Mia had been my friend, though of course, now I realize Mia was actually me—or a splintered fraction of me."

Hanley had wanted to steal my essence with a reaping ceremony, but had failed. His botched attempt had resulted in a small portion of my soul or essence becoming trapped within Hulbetto's Amulet of the Dead.

"Though we are one and the same, Mia developed her own personality and identity separate from mine. For years, she had the ancient collective for company and they influenced who she'd become—who I would become."

"Having that amount of knowledge at your disposal must be incredible."

"They are rather quiet these days."

"I have to tell you, I love your given name, Mia, it suits you."

"I love it, too, and must have subconsciously known it was my real name, but it's also confusing. Who am I? Sarah, Mia, or Charani?"

It wasn't really a question to be answered, so I looked away to scan the grounds. There were a lot of shadows, but nothing ominous. A strange feeling had come over me just then—a prickly sensation I'd felt on numerous occasions.

I wondered, an omen for bad things to come?

"Charani, there's something we need to talk about," Dreah said with obvious trepidation.

"You know you can tell me anything, right?"

"I do. There was more to that vision earlier. I'd already seen the whole thing and so I knew where to stop it."

"Oh?" Now it was my turn to answer with trepidation.

"There are some things you need to know. Unbelievable things that will affect the entire dragon race."

She was hesitant to tell me, but I could see she was determined to do so anyway.

"Some of the things that have to do with Sterling. I'll wait to see if he tells you himself. But, Charani, your father Kristóf...he was...well, he was a Druid."

"What! How can that be? I don't understand."

"Well, I don't profess to understand either, but I'll tell you what I know from the vision. Kristóf was a Druid and Júlia was a Phoenix Dragon, but they were most definitely mated. I think there's more to this, or I sensed as much from the vision. Do you think that if you were in the dreaming, you could connect with the collective better? I mean they are still with you in essence, literally *in essence*!"

She smiled at her joke and I did too. But I wondered if I could. Occasionally, one of the voices of the collective would tell me something, but mostly we were fully integrated with no separation between us. There was no warring for control over my mind or my soul. I was the only one in charge and the only consciousness inhabiting my body and mind.

"I'd be willing to try. The dreaming has been quiet, not

that I'm complaining. I do find a few voices in there, but mostly just my demons."

I didn't have to explain because Dreah understood the impact of those demons all too well. She had her own that loved to haunt her in the dreaming. Sometimes, I wish I didn't have to sleep and therefore dream. But no matter how hard I tried to stay awake to avoid them, fatigue always won out.

"I'll try now, there are hours to go before dawn. Maybe one of the ancient dragons that had been trapped in the amulet can help us to understand what is going on."

"Yes! Be sure to ask them about Druids and Dragons mating. I think this is something that needs to be explored."

I agreed to find out and we walked back to the house together. I hugged her at the top of the steps and we made our way to our rooms.

I rinsed off in a hot shower and then snuggled under the covers. I thought about all the times I had connected with the collective—but before I'd known what they were and what they represented.

Now I actively sought them out as sleep pulled me under. I needed answers and they would be the ones to give them to me. Or so I had thought, but nothing was ever simple, especially while sleeping and floating within the dreaming.

I knew I was dreaming and yet, I was actively manipulating the dreamscape within my mind. I wanted to find one of the ancient dragons that had gifted me with his essence. I needed his knowledge of our ancient dragon history. I needed to know whatever he could tell me about druids and dragons mating.

Some nights when I entered the dreaming, I was pulled directly onto a mission by the voices that found me there. For a change, I created what I wanted, so that I could seek out what I needed.

Tonight my dreaming was beautiful—other times, when my demons lashed out, not so much.

I'd brought my musical shield in with me, hoping to keep the demons at bay. Tonight it was transparent and loosely woven, that way the collective could still reach me through my defensive shield.

Before I'd learned the art of creating my own musical shield for protection, the voices within the dreaming and their pain would force me to shift to shadow. I would follow their unique pain pathway to wherever they were located, usually too late to save them, like poor Ralph and Dreah's mother.

I had virtually no control over shifting this way and quickly realized the inherent danger of *not* being in control. I was thankful Cipriano had taught me how to protect myself. Now I always brought protection in with me, though sometimes my shield didn't work.

When Cipriano visited me within my asylum hell, I thought my dark companion was a figment of my imagination, but he'd been real. He'd saved my life with the colorful stories of his life and his homeland.

My homeland—Scotland.

I wanted to walk along the shore of the deep loch where he'd lived and played as a young boy with his brothers. Where the surface of the water perfectly reflected the blue skies above and the majestic mountains surrounding.

Cipriano created magnificent adventures from his memories of home to divert my attention away from my pain and my desire to fade. He showed me our beautiful homeland and in the process gave me the gift of freedom, if only in my mind.

Through his dragon-eyes and form, we'd traveled over craggy hills and deep glens, his wings stirring the wild grass and purple heather below. We scaled the face of Ben Nevis, a snow capped mountain within the Grampians, and located within the Highlands. We saw wild sheep and goats practically hanging off the steep rocky sides.

I fell in love with Scotland during my dungeon hell. In my heart, it represented freedom and called to my aching soul. It still did. Despite the heartache associated with my homeland, including the loss of Cipriano's brothers, Jakoi and Aiden, his parents and my parents, and my abduction, I thought it was beautiful.

The land wasn't to blame for the sins of man and drampire.

When I entered the dreaming, I went to Scotland to dream and to find answers, I hoped.

I sat on a rock formation that edged the loch and waited. I opened my mind and for good measure—my heart, hoping the collective would hear my pleas and come to chat with me.

I waited and waited, until finally I had to concede defeat. I was disappointed to say the least, but perhaps I couldn't force an encounter and it had to happen more naturally. Deciding to relax and slip into a normal dreaming, I left Scotland and headed to the home within my mind and pictured the estate.

I could feel morning approach but was reluctant to wake and felt safe to slide deeper into sleep. So, I'd inadvertently dropped my guard and that's when it all started. I didn't recognize the insidious attack for what it was...

War!

"Where are you, Soul Seeker? You promised to save her. She came to you. She screamed for you!"

"Dreah? Dreah, where are you honey? I'm here, tell me where you are!"

"She begged for your help, but you ignored her pleas. You heard her, but you didn't listen. Why? Why did you let her mother die? It's all your fault!"

At the center of an immense room was a large rock that looked like a flat cairn. The rock was discolored and deeply stained with the blood of my ancestors, a testament to the atrocities my dragon brethren had suffered.

I was in Hulbetto's warehouse again, reliving the night I found Dreah and her mother—an all too frequent occurrence. The glyph between my shoulders ached and my nose stung with the noxious, stinging scent I'd come to associate with dark magic.

I could feel the echo of pain and suffering. Dreah and her mother, lay immobilized on the rock, but I could no longer feel her mother.

I was too late! I was always too late.

She was littered with more glyphs than I'd ever seen and she'd been brutally eviscerated. The rock bore yet another dragon death. Dreah had several glyphs carved into her delicate skin and each one glowed with dark magic.

She wasn't speaking and her gaze was fixed and staring up at the ceiling. I rushed to her side.

She was dead.

I grabbed Dreah and pulled her into my arms—dropping to my knees. I was an utter failure as a soul seeker. Would I ever be in time?

I wanted to die with Dreah in this moment. I wanted to escape the never-ending struggle. The constant strife and misery. I wanted to make a difference and find the souls that were suffering and deliver them from hell.

My efforts were worthless. I was worthless!

Despair gripped my heart in a brutal vise. I could feel what little hope I had accumulated exsanguinate from my dying soul—one painful drop at a time. I had failed to protect Dreah, failed to save her mother.

Tears slid freely down my face. I wept for this little girl and all that she would miss. I wept for her dreams—never to be realized.

I pulled her limp body tighter against my chest and screamed as loud as I could, "Why!" Not caring who heard my rare outburst.

"Why?" I sobbed softly, my eyes shut tight. Tears escaping to anoint her neck.

"I'm so sorry little one..." I whispered, my voice raspy and small, "so sorry."

With my eyes shut, I didn't see that my aura had surrounded her in the white light of healing. She was alive and I didn't realize it until I heard her weakly within my mind.

"Do not save me," Dreah whispered.

What? No...no that's not right! It didn't happen that way.

I gathered my dragon essence and prepared it for her.

"Drink, little one," I frantically implored, "drink of my essence and be Renascent!"

"No! I refuse your gift! I will not drink. I will not be Renascent. Do not save me! I won't live as a freak!"

"Dreah? What...what do you mean? Drink and be reborn, I beg of you."

I knew this was a dream, but doubted my sanity and my motives. She wanted to be reborn, didn't she? Did I make that up? Had I fabricated her wishes to be reborn?

What have I done?

The nightmare continued and was worse than imaginable...

Dreah opened her solemn amber eyes to look up at me. I would die to protect her.

"I hate you," Dreah told me.

No! Why is it all so different. This isn't right.

I arched my back as I was hit with a burning pain that sliced across my back from left to right in a ripping arc that felt like fire.

"I see you made it in time, well..." Hulbetto said, trailing off with the unsaid implication hanging in the air between us.

He had taken me unawares. Where were all those wonderful dragon senses when I had needed them?

Hulbetto's eyes were glowing green and his smile was evil incarnate. I curled around Dreah, even though this time, she didn't want me or my essence.

Hulbetto licked my blood from where it dripped off the Sword of Dramascus—from Aiden. I refused to answer Hulbetto or cry out. The pain was excruciating, that much was the same.

"My Lady," a voice whispered through my mind, "I cannot control his strikes, no matter my wishes."

I tried to focus on the words, but it was difficult through the haze of pain. Focus, Charani. Focus!

"But I would have forced the killing blow if I could have!" Aiden said in anger.

"Aiden?"

"Aye. You need to die. Don't fight Hulbetto, just die. The clans don't want you. They don't want to be united!"

He faded away and said no more. I was left with a lingering

sense of desolation, but like the real events, I would tether his soul to mine and snatch a remnant before he could disappear.

Hulbetto looked the same and evil still emanated from him and his magic-enriched aura remained muddy, yet it was different. There was a tinge of color, but before I could assess the difference, his apprentice came into view—Damascus arrow notched and ready to fly.

I stared straight into Hulbetto's soul-less eyes and stood unflinching, despite the bone-deep laceration.

Dreah moved away from me instead of towards me. I looked at her, but she looked at Hulbetto. I shook my head confused.

"Did you know that Hulbetto was an anagram for butthole?" I taunted.

His eyes narrowed on me and he struck out, clipping my upper arm and back. He was still pissed at my anagram reference.

I was bleeding from multiple strike points.

My dragon would be so little compared to him, but I shifted

anyway to escape his next blow. The current created by his sword lifted my hair just as I turned to dragon.

Ha! I was a proper-sized dragon this time because I knew what I was doing now. Phoenix or not, I knew how to reach that well of power and tapped into it so that I was big this time and not so small.

An arrow whizzed by my ear. I barrel rolled to my left to miss having my head skewered. Maybe I should have stayed small.

The apprentice; I forgot about the apprentice again!

I pulled my wings in tight and arrowed myself towards him, diverting his course away from Dreah. I pushed at her mind to run out the door, but she didn't move an inch.

The apprentice let fly another arrow.

I changed direction and went straight for Hulbetto. He saw me coming and readied his sword to strike out at me.

I had my ears attuned to the twang of the bowstring releasing.

The arrow that should have buried itself into Hulbetto's

shoulder like before, found its home in mine! I was a bigger target this time and didn't move fast enough or shift to shadow in time.

Weakness, along with my bigger size, added weight to my movements, as did the Damascus steel arrow. The paralysis instituted by the Damascus, steadily crept over my body and forced me to shift.

Hulbetto and Dreah, along with the apprentice stood over my naked body and I knew what was coming.

The killing blow.

Hulbetto had the apprentice carry me over to the sacrificial rock. After kicking Dreah's mother off the cairn, the apprentice proceeded to drop me onto its saturated surface. My blood would join the blood of my brethren, adding to the stains already embedded within.

It had bore witness to the repeated reaping and subsequent deaths of hundreds, upon thousands of dragons over the centuries.

I tried to wake myself, but couldn't. I tried to reinforce my shield, but it was far too late for that. I reminded myself that this wasn't really happening, but the excruciating pain said otherwise.

The events felt real, as if I were experiencing them right now!

"Knowledge is power and you have neither," sneered Hulbetto.

I could have replied, but I refused him my voice.

"You will die here, just as your dragon brethren have over the centuries. There will be no saving the dragons from themselves. You won't release the collective tonight, as you once did. They will remain with me, trapped within the Amulet of the Dead, right where they belong."

Could I really die within the dreaming? Could history be changed?

Hulbetto raised Aiden, my blood still smeared across the steel and I knew this was it.

I looked over to Dreah and tears blurred my vision. Her complexion was sallow and not the healthy glow of youth. Her auburn hair hung listlessly and her amber eyes were vacant.

For her, I would breach my silence, "I love you, Dreah. Thank you for loving me, as a daughter would a mother; and, for being the sister of my heart as you grew older and needed me as your companion."

"I might have dropped a tear for that one," Hulbetto said in disdain.

"I forgive you, Aiden. You are not to blame!" I said, as Hulbetto brought Aiden swiftly down.

1 7

———————

"**M**y Lady! My Lady! Wake up! Wake up, NOW!"

Sputtering and choking, I came awake with a gasp, but as soon as I stopped coughing, I was immediately engulfed in flames.

The wounds I sustained within the dreaming had followed me here and hurt like hell! My bed was saturated with both the ice water Violet had just thrown in my face and the blood from my injuries.

"What happened, Violet?"

"I don't know. I was forced to shift when you drifted into a deeper, yet restless sleep. It didn't feel natural. Did you take some kind of hallucinogen, My Lady?"

"No. At least not that I'm aware of."

I shifted to a small version of my Phoenix, hoping to heal my injuries. When I shifted back, the burning had lessened, but wasn't entirely gone.

"Here, let me help you, as you once helped me," Violet said before whispering something in a language I didn't understand.

"Thank you. I didn't know that you could heal people, Violet."

"You did most of it yourself, I merely accelerated what you had already started on your own."

The pain had definitely subsided after she whispered over my injury.

"Can you tell me what happened now?"

"I need to see Dreah right now. Do you want to shift to ink before I call her to come to me?"

"No, we need to meet and now is the time," Violet replied simply.

It was her decision. It had been years, but I was glad they would finally meet. I sent a call out to Dreah and knew that she'd be here within moments. She'd known what I was going to attempt. But neither of us could have predicted what would occur once I was within the dreaming.

She knocked on my bedroom door, but only came in when I bade her enter. She took one look at my face, saw the bloody bed and ran to me—throwing her arms around me and squeezing me desperately.

The residual pain of that alternate Dreah faded to nothing. Its weak hold couldn't survive in the face of such love.

"I'm okay!" I said, hugging her back just as fiercely, despite the pain of the wound across my back. It was fading, too.

"Oh God, what happened? You were just supposed to try to talk to the collective. Have they gone all wack-a-doodle?"

"Wack-a-doodle?" I laughed.

"Hey, that's the best I could do, I'm upset! You're hurt and I can feel it," she said, her tears making her voice sound hoarse.

"I'm okay, really. I'll be fine."

"Charani?" She asked with shy inquiry "Did you know you had a faery sitting on your flowers?"

I looked over to Violet and burst out laughing. The expression on her face was comical. She was perched on top of my wild daisies looking everywhere, but at the two of us—and whistling.

"Did you accidentally pick her up, when you were picking your flowers?"

Now it was Violet's turn to laugh and it was so beautifully melodic that Dreah and I stopped laughing just to listen her. Once we all settled, I introduced the two of them and surprisingly, Violet explained how we had first met.

"Charani saved your life, Violet," Dreah said, "just as she saved mine and so many others. She doesn't realize the gift that she is."

"That is so true. So we will continue to remind her until she realizes her worth."

"Okay. Enough you two, I'm right here," I said, rolling my eyes, "let's get down to the business at hand," I finished.

I explained to Dreah and Violet what had happened within the dreaming. How I relived rescuing Dreah and releasing the collective, only this time everything had been different—flipped upon itself and opposite.

"It was like someone was manipulating me within the dreaming, as if they could alter the original memory to reflect what they wanted. How could that be possible?"

"Did you learn anything? Did you have a chance to chat with the collective?" Dreah asked.

"No, I never did." I turned to Violet and said, "I would have died within the dreaming, I'm sure of it. Thank you for waking me, Violet, and for not drowning me in the process."

"Ha," she burst out with her tinkling laughter, "I was just returning the favor, My Lady, from when you first found me and nearly drowned me with your tears."

She explained to Dreah how I had nearly drowned her and we both laughed. Though recalling how I found her was sobering and so was the flipped memory.

"You're welcome and I do think you are correct about the dreaming. You sustained injuries there and they followed you here. Plus, you were bleeding from those injuries while you were laying in your bed—dreaming."

"How in the hell is that even possible?"

I just couldn't wrap my brain around any of this, and I was having a hard time with the implications. But as I reasoned out various explanations, one thing that kept coming back to me. What if this was how the dragons and our brethren were being attacked?

"Do you guys think that the drampires are somehow

manipulating us within the dreaming? Altering our perceptions and killing us when we're vulnerable and unable to protect ourselves? How could they do that?"

"With a very rare ability used by a Morpheus Dragon," Cipriano said as he walked into my bedroom.

Violet flew up to Cipriano and gave him a rare caress to his cheek, "My Lord, I am so happy to see you. We are in need of your guidance."

"So good to see you, too, Violet," he told her with genuine affection and then with a pointed look in my direction, he said, "And thank you for reaching out to me."

I shrugged my shoulders. I would have told him what was going on—eventually. I was still trying to shake the hold that altered reality had on my emotions.

"Tell me what happened."

I went over the altered memory again for his benefit. I left nothing out, not even the part with Aiden. Cipriano needed to know everything that occurred so that we could figure out what was happening within the dreaming.

I would rather take on my demons, every day and twice on Sunday, over having to deal with another flipped memory. It had left me emotionally drained.

Dreah and Violet were sitting together by the windows with Violet sitting in Dreah's palm. Another wave of peace drifted through my unsettled heart as I watched them getting to know each other.

Dreah's excitement and animation as she chatted quietly

with Violet, helped to dispel the lingering effects from that flipped memory. The vision of Dreah's vacant eyes and sallow complexion were fading and my heart sighed in relief. They were gradually replaced by the beautiful and vibrant —real Dreah.

I watched Violet wrap Dreah's long auburn hair around her shoulders and whisper, "I've wanted to touch your hair for years! 'Tis beautiful, *lille venn.*"

Dreah smiled shyly at Violet's comment. They were going to be the best of friends that much was evident. Violet had come to know Dreah through me and had watched her grow and mature into the beautiful and gracious young woman that she was today.

Returning my gaze to Cipriano, I asked, "Could this Morpheus Dragon invade Dreah's dreams as well?"

"I think so. She had dragon essence flowing in her veins before you ever gifted her with some of yours."

"Did I gift it to her, Cipriano? Or did I force it upon her? By intervening in her life, did I alter who and what she would have become?"

I turned away from the concern in Cipriano's grey eyes. These questions were tearing me up. I couldn't shake the vile doubt from toying with my mind. The idea that I may have hurt Dreah by giving her my dragon essence made me physically nauseous.

"Charani?" I heard Dreah say, just before she stepped in front of me.

"Look at me," she instructed, as if I were a child to be coddled, "Are you looking at me?" she asked.

"You can see that I am," I replied a little miffed, as the anguish from the damned dream kept ripping through me. But I stared into her amber eyes and listened to what she had to say.

"Are you, Charani? Do you see me? I mean really see me? I'm not the Dreah from your flipped dream. I'm *your* Dreah, just as I've been since the moment you stormed into Hulbetto's warehouse."

She reached out to grab my hand, her ring warming under my touch.

"I've been yours since you saved my life and became my mother. All in an instant! There was no question or indecision on your part. You would be a mother to me and that was the end of it. And I have loved you ever since that moment and will never stop."

Her words were replacing the doubt.

"May I tell you what I have found to be the most astonishing thing of all?"

"You never have to ask, Dreah. You can tell me anything and everything."

Dreah and I had always been close. I made sure to foster an open relationship with her so she would feel comfortable sharing her thoughts and her feelings with me.

"You were the perfect mother, Charani. But what I find amazing is that you had no role model to emulate, no bastion of motherhood that you could refer back to as a point of refer-ence. No, you had to figure it out all on your own.

"You made sure that I felt loved and wanted. You encour-aged my inquisitive nature. You taught me that being different was okay and that we should celebrate who and what we are. Now, hold onto my ring and *see* what *I* see!"

I held on as Dreah pulled me into a vision and opened my eyes in an unexpected way.

18

"That's how I saw things that night. Granted some of the events are missing. But from the moment you held me in your arms—until today, that is how I see you," she told me.

Her vision was a montage of me through the years. It was so strange to see myself through her eyes. I didn't recognize the person she showed me in those vignettes. I wasn't heroic, like she had portrayed. I failed all the time and I'd failed her when she needed me the most.

"It's not your fault that she died. Please, let that go. I've never blamed you and you shouldn't blame yourself or hold yourself accountable. That was all Hulbetto and his apprentice—not you."

"I know you're right, but you should've had your real mother to raise you, not a surrogate..."

I could hear the tears in her voice as she interrupted me

with her passionate reply, "You have never been a surrogate, a facsimile or anything other than my mother—plain and simple! I know we've transitioned to a sister-like relationship, but you will always be my mother."

"Come here," I said opening my arms.

We held each other in unconditional love and under-standing. We were both orphaned and as such, we'd adopted each other. The dream-Dreah faded and disappeared in the presence of *my* Dreah.

"Okay, down to the business at hand," I said.

Cipriano and Violet had been speaking quietly with one another, giving Dreah and I a small measure of privacy while we had our moment. They walked back over to join us, Violet sitting on Cipriano's shoulder.

"Violet and I were talking about your altered dream. What if your idea is right? What if drampires really are invading the dreaming to attack dragons while they are asleep and vulnerable?"

"It would explain a lot. Dragons aren't exactly helpless creatures. But there would be no way to anticipate such an insidious attack and one so stealthily orchestrated."

"Exactly! I think a Morpheus Dragon must have been captured by a drampire. What if that dragon's essence was stripped and their gift of dreams stolen? That could be the root cause for all of our problems."

"So drampires sneak into the dreaming to find dragons they can manipulate and ultimately kill. Stealing their essence to fuel their immortality. It makes sense, but if we're right, how in the world do we prevent them from doing so?"

"We make protective amulets and fight them at their own game," Dreah said.

"Like the ones you made for us?"

"Yes, similar to our family amulets. I would need to create all new ones and for every dragon at sanctuary."

"Dreah you cannot do this on your own. That is far too many amulets for one person."

"I'll have Kestrel, Dusky, and Lyan, help me."

"Count me in as well," Violet said.

OVER THE NEXT WEEK, the five of them worked tirelessly to create enough amulets for everyone, a daunting task. They worked well together and the witches had welcomed Violet into their midst, as if they'd been friends for years.

Every night, Violet would return to rest upon my skin, just as she had for years. I would miss her terribly when she was ready to live beyond this existence we had created with each other.

I sensed there was more to why she stayed with us. But I would keep her for as long as she wanted to stay. But when she was finally ready to address the abuse she had suffered, I would be there for her—no questions asked. I wanted to meet her abuser so I could dish out a little dragon vengeance.

While the girls worked their magic, Cipriano and I spent our time in meetings with clan leaders. We explained what we thought might be happening and our concern for their clansmen. Most of the leaders had agreed that there would be no harm in wearing the amulets, especially if they would help to protect their clans. But, not all of them were convinced and a couple had outright refused.

Stubborn old coots!

We couldn't force them to wear the amulets, just as we couldn't force them to participate and interact with the other clans. Their ancient ways and stagnate ideas were exhausting.

"I only want to protect your people and the dragon race as a whole. Do you want the drampires to win?" I practically yelled one day, not my finest moment, but I'd been beyond frustrated.

The clan leaders were my elders, by centuries, and I had to remind myself of that every time they were being obstinate. They'd seen centuries come and go, which gave them a unique perspective on life, albeit backwards and not very forward thinking.

I was thankful I could seek expert guidance from Cipriano, Ian and Isabella, the twins, and the collective. Although, the collective had been suspiciously quiet when I'd sought them out within the dreaming.

Had the collective been there after all? Were they invisible and inaccessible to me because the drampire had manipulated my perceptions while within the dreaming?

What other dreams or memories had been altered by malicious manipulations? Would I ever know the truth?

Dreah reached out and asked me to come to Kestrel's home where they had been creating the amulets. She said they needed me for the final step and activation of the amulets.

I wasn't sure how I could help, I didn't know the first thing about spelling, or, casting magic. I would do whatever it took to keep sanctuary safe—except what they asked me to do.

19

Dreah, Violet, and the witches were beyond exhausted from creating hundreds of amulets to protect the clansmen while they were asleep and vulnerable within the dreaming. Similar to the amulets Dreah had created for the family, these would prevent manipulation of the clans while they were fast asleep.

At least, that is what we hoped they would do.

"No, Dreah, I can't do it! Anything but that. I did it for the family, but I don't know about this."

The dejected look on her face nearly ripped my heart out. I was willing to do a lot of things to protect our race, but providing my blood *and* my essence to activate all those amulets...

"Isn't there another way to make them work? Can't you do some fancy spelling?" I asked in desperation.

"We've done everything that we could. It has to be *your*

blood and *your* essence. As the last true Phoenix, you are the only one capable of providing the necessary ingredients to make them function."

She gave me a look that said it all, but she sent me a private message as well, *"We must have your druid and dragon blood, as well as the essence of your Phoenix. It's the only way to protect the clans, or so we hope."*

The amulets were laid out, row upon endless row, seeming to go on forever, though I know they didn't. Each one had been intricately created and molded, just like my amulet from Dreah, but that's where the similarities ended.

Shocked by what I saw, I asked in stuttering disbelief, "Are those...glyphs etched onto the surface of a...of a bloodstone?"

Dreah, Violet, Kestrel, Dusky and Lyan, looked at me wide-eyed and mute, but nodded their heads in unison.

"How in the bloody hell do I convince any of the clan leaders to wear these?"

Unfortunately, not all the clansmen were willing to trust us and refused to wear the amulets. They told me that they were too reminiscent of Hulbetto's Amulet of the Dead and they couldn't bring themselves to wear it. Basically, they were choosing to risk death than trust that we only had their safety in mind.

If they all knew how we had created them, none of them would have worn the amulets. I had conceded to Dreah's request, how could I not? She said donating my mixed blood and the essence from my Phoenix was integral to preventing the drampires from invading our dreams.

"If you don't help, Charani, I fear the consequences will be grave."

"Tell me what I need to do."

"Gather your essence and concentrate it within your hand," she told me.

I did as she asked, the blue iridescence of my dragon essence blended with the red of my Phoenix.

"Now," she said, as she cleared her throat and handed me a ceremonial knife, "you have to slice your palm with this Damascus blade."

Taking the knife by the hilt, I ran it across my palm in a deep slice that felt like acid and fire all at once—my breath caught in pain. It would be a permanent mark and we both knew it.

"I'm so sorry," Dreah said, ignoring the tears that dripped from her lashes, "we're almost done."

"Wait!" Violet yelled out.

"Bleeding to death here!"

"Hushy," she said "Dreah, gather your tears and add them to My Lady's blood."

Dreah did as she was told and gathered her tears to sprinkle over my bloody palm.

"Now, rub your hands together."

My hands were glowing, as was the blood and tear

mixture. My palm stung like hell, but I was ignoring it as best I could. I'd suffered worse.

Dreah and the witches began whispering a spell in a language I didn't understand, though it was hauntingly beautiful. Violet added her lyrical voice to the spelling and once I caught on to the repetitive words, I leant my voice as well.

The blood accumulated and was contained within a glowing sphere I had created with my hands. It was about the size of a basketball. I looked to Dreah to see what I was supposed to do now.

The glyph between my shoulder blades was itching, as it responded to the dark magic we were creating for the light purposes of safety and protection. Would there be consequences besides the physical one that I would forever bear?

"Saturate the surface of every amulet with the mixture," Dreah told me and demonstrated what she wanted me to do.

Following her example, I bathed every bloodstone with my blood, my dragon essence, and Dreah's tears. We watched mesmerized, as the thirsty bloodstones soaked up every single drop.

The stones made multiple color transitions, from a glowing dragon blue, to a deep blackish-red, to bright white, but finally settled on magenta.

Each one was luminescent and lit the room in a soft light. I heard a gasp and looked for the source and saw that it was Dreah.

"What, honey? What's the matter?"

"Look upon the surface of every single stone," she said with awe.

When I did, it was my turn to gasp. I hadn't noticed the actual surface of the stones through the glow. The glyphs that had originally been etched into the surface of each bloodstone was gone. They had been replaced by a crystalline teardrop, *Dreah's* teardrop.

Bending to inspect them closer, I noticed that each tear was lined in Phoenix red and each teardrop glowed from within with dragon blue—the source of the luminescence.

"That is amazing! Did you know this would happen, Violet?"

"No, My Lady, but 'tis wondrous and beautiful."

"That it is. It has to work, how could it not with all the potential magic sitting there. Plus, to me, it looks as if my Phoenix is sheltering your tears, Dreah—protecting them."

"Yes, just as you do every day, Charani. You protect and serve the dragon culture—selflessly, and they could all learn by your example."

"Thank you, Dreah, but I wouldn't hold your breath, they are extremely resistant to change."

Our worse fears would be realized and sanctuary would suffer in the aftermath.

2 0

All the dragons currently inhabiting sanctuary were gathered around the new dragon fountain. Cipriano had it commissioned to resemble the one we all loved so much at the estate in Kansas City. I had yet to see the fountain or its statue because Cipriano had hidden it under a thick, dark canvas.

We had it installed at the center of the community square, hoping it would function as a focal point and a meeting place for the clansmen to gather and get to know one another. But, if no one else appreciated the fountain's calming beauty, I knew the family would and that was enough.

We were unveiling both the fountain and the name of sanctuary today. Dreah had named sanctuary years ago when we chose this site to build it upon. How different the area looked today than the day I found Violet. Her pain had been a beacon drawing me to her and this spot.

It was destined to be—finding Violet and therefore, discovering sanctuary.

When planning sanctuary, we decided to keep the area very nature centric. With that in mind, the various buildings and homes throughout sanctuary had been built with wood logs and stone. We wanted to utilize as many natural elements as we could and they were the compliment to the rustic environment.

Looking over the square, via its wall of windows, was the two-story Great Room. It would function as a neutral gathering place for the clans.

Before I addressed the clansmen, I took a moment to bask in the mid-morning sunshine. Though it had been years since my asylum confinement, I still craved wide-open spaces and light—I couldn't get enough light. Sunlight or moonlight, it didn't matter, I found an excuse to be outside every single day or night.

Twenty deep breaths later, I stepped onto the pedestal of the fountain so that I could be seen and heard by everyone.

"Thank you for joining us today and thankfully, the Missouri weather has cooperated. If nothing else, you'll learn that our weather is fickle. If you wait five minutes, it's likely to change."

Lord, I thought that might get at least a little response, a small smile, but nope, nothing at all. My family giggled at my attempts to be funny, but they didn't count, though their support was appreciated.

"I'm Charani, in case you didn't already know that. We created sanctuary for the express purpose of protecting you and the dragon clans. Our culture and our very future are in jeopardy, especially with drampires devising new and inventive ways to kill us and steal our dragon essence to fuel their hijacked immortality."

No one said a word—tough crowd!

"Sanctuary is our home. We hope that one day it will feel like home to you, too, as well as the next generation. Dragons were gifted with the ability to shift into multiple forms, we are long-lived and occasionally, we're immortal. We are strong on our own. But, imagine how much stronger we could be if all the individual clans would come together to unite and become one overarching clan."

The clansmen's attentiveness had shifted. Encouraged, I continued, "If we are to survive and to thrive, we *must* come together. My desire and hope is for dragons to find happiness and tranquility here." With that said, I removed the dark canvas from covering the fountain, the statue, and the inscription with the name of sanctuary.

I would have fallen and made a complete ass of myself if Cipriano hadn't been standing right next to me when I removed the canvas. I looked at the statue at a loss for words.

"You designed this?" I whispered to Cipriano

"We all did," he said, looking over to the family.

They were watching me and my reaction, smiling with

love and happiness. Turning back to the statue, I took a moment to collect myself before continuing to speak to the crowd.

The fountain had two copper dragons—my Phoenix and my hatchling.

The larger, Phoenix Dragon, had been captured and immortalized mid-launch. Her wings were wide-spread and her head held high as she sought the freedom of the sky.

My hatchling was leaning against my statue's hind leg with her wings tucked and her eyes wide, looking up to my Phoenix in—wonder. The name and inscription, etched into the copper base, were perfect, just like the statue. Humbled didn't begin to cover what I was feeling. I sent my family waves of gratitude.

Everlasting: The home of the dragon and the hope for the future.

I cleared my throat, several times, "In a few months, we'll be celebrating the first known dragon birth in centuries, besides mine, and it'll be right here, at Everlasting."

There was clapping and cheering. I had a feeling that Ian and Isabella's child was going to be spoiled rotten with all the "aunts and uncles" running around Everlasting. I couldn't wait to meet him, or, her.

Their child would bring the clansmen together as nothing else could have. It was a joyous occasion and we hoped this birth would entice the mated dragons that were still in hiding to come to Everlasting. I felt they were in danger, especially given what we knew about drampires invading our dreaming.

"So today we celebrate the naming of Everlasting and the next generation of dragons. And, we also wanted to give all of you a gift of protection."

"We think we've discovered how the drampires continue to kill our brethren. They do it within the dreaming," Cipriano explained.

There was a collective gasp at the idea of being attacked when asleep and vulnerable.

"It's cowardly, to say the least," I continued.

Looking over the crowd of people, I saw DeChadik. His blonde hair and height set him apart from his clan. They had been at Everlasting for some time now. This was the first time I'd seen them, though DeChadik seemed to be everywhere and chatting with everyone.

Perhaps he would help us bridge this gap between the various clans. He was very charming and social and people gravitated to those traits.

Sterling was at the back of the crowd leaning up against a tree with his arms crossed—a lone sentinel, watchful and protective. He'd been helpful to Tarrin and Tauric with organizing and training the elite guard for their duties in and around Everlasting.

Brother, my heart whispered with suppressed longing. I

wasn't ready to tell him, not yet. But, could he not recognize himself in me?

"We have created protective amulets for everyone to wear. They should block drampires from invading our dreams and prevent their ability to manipulate us while we are asleep and within the dreaming," Cipriano continued to explain.

The family stepped forward with the new amulets dangling from their hands. We knew some would think they resembled the Amulet of the Dead, though they didn't. The problem stemmed from what the amulets had represented in their minds—the reaping of our dragon essence.

I raised the amulet Dreah handed me high above my head for everyone to see and waited for their reactions. I prayed they could see these anew and let go of the past stigma.

In the sunlight, the unique magenta color of the amulet was stunning. But the crystalline teardrop, glowing with the iridescence of our dragon blue and cradled within the circle of my Phoenix red, was truly magical. After a moment or two, I placed the amulet around my neck to rest next to the one Dreah had created for the family, not that they could see that one.

Following Violet's instructions from last night, I placed an amulet around the neck of each person in my family. She said I had to be the one to place the amulets around each and every person to have the best results. She thought it would make for a magical connection.

The symbolism conveyed trust on their part and protection on mine.

It was daunting to have so many putting their trust in me. Doubt was my constant companion, but I ignored it and placed an amulet on everyone that would accept one.

Sterling was the last one to come forward and unlike any of the other men, knelt before me and placed his fist over his heart—waiting. I was stunned at what this represented, like knights of old, he was offering his fealty—to me.

My family and the collective had done the same and this was no less humbling.

My brother knelt before me and he had no idea. Tears clogged my throat, but I couldn't afford to let them loose.

"Please, Sterling, stand up." I asked, as I reached out to hold his hand.

I cleared my throat of emotion and placed the amulet around his awaiting neck.

"Thank you for the support you have given Everlasting. You have been instrumental in the development and training of the elite guard. You've helped to make our dragon brethren safer in their new homes."

I wondered if he could feel the familial bond of brother and sister as I held his hand. I'd quickly reinforced my shield to prevent my emotions from spilling out. He didn't give any indication that he'd felt anything, which was good since I wasn't ready.

"I'm honored to have been included in the process. Thank you for the protective amulet. I promise to always wear it," he told me, as if he were saying goodbye.

"Are you leaving, Sterling?"

"Not yet, but I do want to relocate my small clan here."

21

The Great Room was packed with dragons from the various clans, a shocking display of support for a dragon who wasn't a part of their own clan. Four of DeChadik's clansmen had been murdered by drampires and we were holding a memorial in their honor.

A night of remembrance, similar to what we did for Dreah's parents. Tonight's celebration of life was working to unite the clans, like nothing else had. All the clans could relate to his grief. They'd all lost someone, whether to life's passage or to the drampires, it didn't matter.

At some point in life, loss and grief visits everyone. It's merely a matter of *when* it will come—not *if*.

"It's unfortunate," I told Cipriano, "that it took the death of more dragons to solidify the purpose of Everlasting. The clans surprised me, though, and have risen to the occasion.

They came together to support DeChadik as he mourns the loss of his clansmen."

Their bodies had been found eviscerated and covered in glyphs and miles from Everlasting. The elite dragon guard had found them while on patrol, hanging from an ancient Oak tree— by their protective amulets.

The symbolism of the ritual had not been lost on any of us. The fact drampires used an Oak tree to hang the two men and two women from, was an affront to our cultural beliefs.

In dragon legend, the Oak tree represents safety and hospitality; provides protection for our dragon leaders and warriors; as well as being the mystical symbol of truth and bravery.

They brutally murdered our brethren. They desecrated that ancient Oak.

"Yes," Cipriano agreed, "and it was the heinous act of a coward."

I was furious and yet, helpless as to what to do.

"This was a great idea to bring everyone together. Even the older dragons are here and interacting with the others."

The older dragons and surprisingly, some of the newer ones, had been slow to embrace change or rather, too much change. I had to give them credit though, they had moved their clansmen to the Ozarks. They came for the idea of protection in numbers, but despite that, they had remained fragmented—much to my frustration.

There had been minimal interactions between clans,

except for the dragons that were in our elite guard. There, they had a mutual goal and a mission to complete. They patrolled Everlasting and it was through this common purpose that they'd become comrades-in-arms.

If only the remaining dragons would follow suit. A few of the women came to the weekly defense lessons, but only a few. The majority remained segregated, refusing to venture past their clans' territory within Everlasting.

The witches came every week to train with Dreah and I. It always made for a good time, especially when their familiars came along to play.

Isabella wasn't currently participating in any of the activities that required shifting because when female dragons were expecting, they weren't able to shift. They remained in human form until after their child was safely delivered. This made them vulnerable and Ian was more than a little stressed about her inability to shift.

We were all taking turns protecting Isabella. She hated us hovering, so we tried to be stealth-like, but we weren't fooling her. Ian and Isabella were rarely separated and were a great example to the dragons living at Everlasting. They were actively involved in bringing the clans together and would visit everyone on a regular basis.

"I want to thank every single one of you for coming tonight in support of DeChadik."

Looking about the room, I made eye contact with every

person there before I continued. I wanted them to know I saw them and, they would see me.

"His loss is our loss; his clan was our clan; because ultimately, we are one. We are different and with unique abilities, which we should celebrate."

I looked pointedly at the old ones, as they were so worried about losing their identities.

"Our histories make us who and what we are, but I will tell you one very important fact that unites each and every one of us." Before I continued, I waited to be sure I had their full and undivided attention.

"We. Are. Dragon!"

Heads were nodding, even the old ones.

"Never doubt that's what will unite us—what will prevent us from being torn asunder. We will prevail over the drampires. They will not win. I implore you to keep wearing your protective amulets. We know they will work. The drampires somehow orchestrated it to appear as if they don't. They want our complacency. Don't give it to them. Rise above the doubt."

A few that weren't wearing their amulets, slipped them back around their necks. My heart soared with the implications, they were trusting in us, in me, and in Everlasting.

Fate was a fickle bitch and trust was hard to keep, especially when half-truths were mixed with lies to taint the truth and cast doubt upon the message.

22

Over the past week, we'd definitely seen an improvement in clan relations and tonight's celebration was a way to build on that momentum and progress. One thing I'd learned from my adoptive parents, Sebastian and Helena, was the benefit of bringing people together for a mutual cause.

Tonight's purpose was to celebrate Everlasting. I was determined to unite the dragons in purpose—protection of *their* clans and of the dragon race as a whole, especially in the wake of the devastating loss of DeChadik's clansmen. That was a serious blow to the idea we were a safe haven for dragons.

I felt responsible for their deaths, even though we were doing everything we could think of to protect every dragon here at Everlasting.

I should have felt them. I should have known they were in

danger, but I'd been deaf to their cries and insensate to their pain.

I was failing my race as the last true Phoenix!

DeChadik was helping, where I wasn't, I had to admit. He was quite social and seemed to be everywhere all at once. Plus, the clans were rallying around him in support. It was refreshing to see them coming together—finally.

Despite what happened to DeChadik's clan, most of the clans were still wearing their amulets, though not all. I guess I couldn't blame them for that, but they did work and I'd prove it somehow. But, first I had to figure out why the amulets hadn't protected his clan.

The Great Room was overflowing with food and drinks. Every clan had brought their favorite dishes to share. The delicious aroma from the various spices was truly mouth watering. I'd sampled everything.

One of the Scot's dragons, Janna, had made a thick steak and ale pie with a golden pie crust that had flaked to perfection. It was, by far, my favorite of all the savory dishes.

When I asked her if she would share her secret to the flaky pie crust, not that I liked to bake, she surprised me and happily shared her secret.

"Oh aye. Well ye see," she stopped, looking left and right, she motioned me forward with her finger, then whispered, "I use a wee nip of the vodka. Now mind ye, I tried using the scotch, but it dinna taste proper like," she finished with a sassy wink.

She was a sweet lady and was one of the few clansmen that would socialize with others.

"'Tis right silliness the ole ones be dragging their feet like. 'Tis time to move forward," she told me one day during defense lessons.

I wish everyone felt as she did, it sure would make things easier. Change was painful, I reminded myself for the thousandth time that day.

Cipriano was across the room and alone for the moment. He was leaning against the log wall, a warrior guarding his charges. Grabbing two glasses and a bottle of honey mead off one of the tables, I made way to join him in blessed seclusion, behind the dessert table—perfect.

Handing him a glass of vanilla-spiced honey mead, I smiled at his frequent glances at the dessert table, "Did you try the dessert Kestrel made?" I asked, sipping at my mead, the flavor mellow and soft in my mouth.

"Do you mean the mile-high cake of chocolate perfection? That one?"

Laughing, I replied, "Yes, that one. Who knew witches were such culinary aficionados. Though, I guess it makes total sense. But goodness, it was so creamy, and so rich and delicious."

He laughed, too. It was a nice reprieve to relax for an evening. We were on guard all the time. Looking out over the crowd of people, I saw DeChadik circulating amongst them all, thanking them for their support I would guess.

"I began to wonder if they would remain fragmented forever, despite living together at Everlasting," I said, nodding towards the roomful of clansmen.

"The old ones worry unnecessarily, that they will lose what makes them unique. At this point, if we don't worry about the decimation of the entire dragon race, clan individuality won't matter because we'll be dead," Cipriano said, shaking his head in disappointment.

The continued resistance has been so frustrating—to all of us. It was enough to drive me to drink, though I rarely, if ever did. It was too reminiscent of when I was drugged at the asylum. No, thank you, I like the being in control too much, but one glass of mead would be okay.

Sterling was laughing with Kestrel, Dusky, Lyan, and Dreah. He was eating another helping of the chocolate cake of perfection. I smiled at my brother's sweet tooth. The witches were hanging on his every word. I couldn't blame them for that, Sterling was extremely handsome, with his black hair and blue eyes. But, I thought it might be his reserved countenance that challenged them.

Dreah loved the witches, but she felt protective of Sterling with all the things she knew about his life. Clearly he could take care of himself, however, at the moment she looked like she'd break out her fighting skills to protect his honor and fend the witches off.

Giggling to myself and sipping more of the mead, I saw Ian and Isabella were making the rounds as well. Currently they were speaking with Geoffrey and Alain—the stubborns, I called them, if only in my mind. Isabella dressed in loose dresses and blouses to minimize the size of her growing abdomen and the child within. She was beautiful before, but now, she truly glowed.

Tarrin and Tauric had given the elite guard the night off and were on patrol duty. They wanted their guards to be here for the festivities and to show support for Everlasting and the unification of the clans. Mingling and getting to know the other clansmen was paramount to fostering cooperation and encouraging involvement.

A few of the elite guard had wanted to help with patrol, but the twins were adamant the guards needed to be here. They wanted the guards to set an example of what it meant to participate in something that benefited everyone and not just one clan or another. They were very proud of their guards, as they should be. We all were.

Cipriano and I had remained alone, behind the dessert table, despite being surrounded by hundreds of clansmen, resident witches, and a few other supernatural races that had come to live with us.

"It's time, isn't it?" I asked.

I continued looking out over the crowd because I wouldn't be able to hide my facial expressions when he told me what I already knew was coming.

"It is."

Once I compartmentalized my emotions, I could hide

them behind the thick musical shield I engaged, only then did I trust myself to face Cipriano.

"I've felt the time was near. You've stayed way past the timeframe we'd discussed."

"No, I stayed despite the timeframe *you* wanted, Charani. Aiden could wait, he's been missing a long time. But setting up Everlasting, our sanctuary, could not wait. Too many dragons have died at the hands of drampires and we needed to do something to protect the rest."

There was pain and resignation in his grey eyes, though they were tempered by his determination to complete his journey to recover Aiden and bring him home.

"Aiden needs you now, I can feel it."

"He does. I should have tried to bring the clans together before now but, we needed you; I, needed you, Charani. As the last true Phoenix, none of this would have been possible without you."

For once, I didn't doubt the veracity of that statement. I knew why it was indeed the truth, my druid father and dragon mother made it so. I needed to tell him the truth, but it would keep. He needed to go and I wouldn't influence his leaving by sharing all the new information I'd recently discovered.

Tonight was turning out to be a monumental and pivotal night.

Everlasting was working to fulfill its promise to the dragons living here. It started with the clans' willingness to step beyond themselves to support DeChadik in his time of grief. A sense of community had been fostered in the wake of his clansmen's deaths. Unfortunate, but instrumental in enacting a positive change and a huge step forward.

Why must all forward progress be tempered by the inevitable steps backwards?

Earlier that evening, before the celebration had started, I fortified my protective shield as I played the cello. The notes I created had been woven together to make my shield impenetrable and stronger than ever.

Cipriano was leaving and I didn't want my friend and mentor to know just how much I still needed him. I'd become so adept at hiding my emotions behind my shield, that he had no idea of the doubt and fear that plagued me daily. Or about the demons that still haunted me within the dreaming.

I couldn't tell him. He needed to go. He had to find Aiden before it was too late to save his tortured soul—if it wasn't already too late.

Trapped in the Sword of Dramascus, Aiden had been forced to kill his brethren—for centuries on end, as the drampires' instrument of death.

Hulbetto had wielded Aiden with deadly precision,

forcing him to mortally injure me. Later, Aiden had begged me to tell his brother, Cipriano, to destroy the sword so that he might die as well. I wouldn't allow it and neither would Cipriano.

I didn't understand how or why I did this, but I had tethered both Aiden and Rowan, to my soul for safekeeping. Rowan, when I was a child of eight, and Aiden, twice.

I dreamt of them often, both suffering unspeakably, but they were too far away for me to find and to save.

Soul Seeker, my ass!

"Sister, what has you frowning?"

Surprised, I looked up. Searching his face and his emotions, I was shocked to see that he really couldn't feel me and yet, I could feel him.

"Nothing. I will miss you, my brother, but bring him home."

"I'll try. I've been searching for him these long centuries and I won't give up until he's found. That apprentice took him from Hulbetto's warehouse. I'll start by looking for him."

"I saw that apprentice in Dreah's vision. I watched him kill Kristóf with his damned crossbow and Damascus arrow."

I projected the picture I had of the apprentice to Cipriano's mind one more time, just in case. After my recent nightmare where everything had been flipped upon itself, I had a clearer picture of him.

I would eventually hunt him down and kill him, I vowed it!

I still hadn't shared my familial revelations with Cipriano. He didn't know that Sterling was my brother and neither did Sterling. Kristóf and Júlia were my parents and neither one of them knew that either. Dreah knew and she was keeping it to herself. I was still trying to process it all and doing a poor job of it.

"You'll keep in touch, won't you?" I asked.

I couldn't bear to be without Cipriano. He was my brother, my mentor, and like a father to me. I was so thankful that I would be able to feel him through our connection. I would always know where he was and if he was okay.

"I can feel your worry, Charani. I'll be fine and I will stay connected with you and the family—no matter the distance."

"I know you will. Now is a great time to go. Everything is settling down and the clans are finally working together."

"Yes and I will leave them in your very capable hands. You are a born leader, though you don't feel it's so, I know it is. The clans will come together and you will lead them into a brighter future—as one united clan."

"You, my friend, have been drinking too much wine!" I smiled and laughed, hoping to hide my rising fear of failing.

"Come here, sister," he said, and pulled me into his arms.

It felt like we were in a bubble of isolation, so I allowed myself to sink into his warm embrace. I captured this rare moment to cherish for eternity.

Once I realized that my room had been compromised at Everlasting, it was far too late to save myself.

I couldn't wake from the dreaming fast enough and consequently, I was far too slow to react and my betrayers were able to secure my wrists with shackles made from ancient Damascus.

Instantly I could feel the paralysis creep up my arms and take over my body.

When I was asleep and within the dreaming, I became deeply immersed within my nightmares—completely trapped and remembering. I relived every heinous moment of what should have been my final internment within Dr. Hanley's asylum basement.

The degradation and helplessness I felt, along with the inevitability and acceptance of my impending death, had been the absolute lowest point of my life.

Despair had eroded all my hope—I hit rock bottom and had given up the will to live.

Those flashbacks loved to chase me down and haunt me. They were like a cancer eliciting doubt within my mind and my emotional progress suffered accordingly. However, I refused to let them take root and metastasize, instead, I used them to illustrate to myself just how far I'd come since my death and rebirth.

In the wake of my nightmares, I'd throw open all the windows to clear the stinging scent of fear from my room. It clung tenaciously to everything, including my skin, which felt coated in its filth.

I kept those nightmares to myself and stuffed them behind the musical shield I created to hide things from my family. I couldn't bear to see their pity. Perhaps if I'd shared my burden with them, the strength of my nightmares would have diminished and I wouldn't be wearing shackles now and paralyzed mute.

While I was still capable of looking about my room, I looked at each clansman that had dared to breach my space. I watched as they shifted from shadow to human form and I wasn't at all surprised by a few that I saw, but completely shocked by others.

Though change was inevitable in life, it was generally considered to be quite painful, but especially for those clans mired in centuries of tradition. For them, it was proving to be excruciating. But, I wouldn't have believed they'd turn against me—the creator of Everlasting.

Secrets always manage to find the light of day and mine were no exception.

I refused to open my mind to my family and call for help. I wouldn't endanger them, but I would protect them with my very life.

I was alone and my betrayers had known as much. Cipriano had finally left to search for Aiden. Dreah was visiting with the witches. The twins were on patrol and Ian had taken Isabella to the estate in Kansas City.

Perfect timing.

By the time we left my room, I was no longer able to walk. The Damascus steel had worked just as they knew it would, paralyzing my muscles.

DeChadik carried me outside where everyone quickly shifted into their dragon forms. The static electricity from so many shifting at once, made my hair stand on end.

DeChadik.

If I hadn't already been paralyzed, the shock of his betrayal would have finished the job. But, I understood. When his clansmen had needed me the most, I failed them. They were dead because I didn't hear their cries for help. It was my responsibility as their Phoenix, to protect them and it was no wonder that he blamed me—I blamed myself.

Heedless of how his talons would dig into my skin,

DeChadik grabbed me hard and launched us into the sky to follow the others.

There wasn't a damned thing I could do about what was happening and my mind screamed in denial. I was resolute in one thing—I'd made a promise to myself after my rescue from the asylum: I would never willingly submit to imprisonment again. Once had been enough.

Despite being immortal, I'd find a way to transition to the other side before I spent years imprisoned and I didn't care what that said about me.

But first, I would fight. I wasn't willing to give up without looking for a way out of this situation.

We didn't fly for very long before we landed. I was dropped to the ground at DeChadik's feet as he shifted back to his human form. I glared up at him, but the sentiment was wasted as I couldn't cock my eyebrow to get a proper glare going.

He carried me through the entrance of the cave before us. There were probably a thousand such caves located throughout the Ozarks. Some of these ancient caves would travel deep into the earth, such as this one.

The winding path through the cave, narrowed and shortened the deeper we went. Sharp rocks encroached upon the pathway making it treacherous. At least I could see in the dark this time or could use my dragon essence to illuminate the space around me.

Once we were deep underground, he walked into a rock enclosed cell and dropped me onto the dirt floor. After removing the shackles, he stepped back and closed the door behind him. The bars to the cell and the door were made of Damascus.

I wouldn't be able to get past those bars, but at least my whole body wouldn't continue to be paralyzed from the shackles.

No one said a thing. Not one word. I had no idea what was going on, but eventually they would tell me. Maybe they'd chat after I got my voice back. Not that I'd use it.

I learned the power of withholding my voice the last time my freedom had been stolen from me. I'd gone years without speaking a single syllable. I would do it again, if for no other reason than to infuriate my captors and prevent them from attaining whatever it was they wanted.

My immediate goal: frustrate them into action.

DeChadik and the clansmen left me laying on my side on the dirt floor, still paralyzed from the effects of the Damascus shackles. Unable to move, I remained where I'd been dropped, and stared through the bars of my new prison.

The claustrophobic weight of the cave pressed upon me making it difficult to breathe.

I'd been trapped before in a dungeon and awaiting a death sentence, only this time I could see in the dark, but it didn't help. I was still afraid to close my eyes. I feared the demons that continued to haunt my nightmares would chase me down and destroy what was left of my fortitude.

Fatigue won the battle. I was pulled directly under and thrust straight into them. Despite their frequency, I wasn't prepared for the emotional devastation of reliving those nightmares yet again and with such clarity...

I DROPPED RIGHT into the moment when a little boy had irrevocably changed the course of my life.

My adoptive parents were hosting one of their many charity fundraisers that night. I'd come downstairs to play the piano for their guests when a wave of paralyzing emotion had rendered me frozen in abject fear.

His fear, though, and not my own.

He'd come screaming through my mind and marked my soul indelibly with his. The dissonance of his cries continued to echo through my mind until I wept from the raw emotions.

Years later, I still couldn't shake the feeling that I had somehow failed that little boy—even though I'd only been a child myself.

As an eight-year-old child and even now, as an adult, it was incomprehensible the torture he endured. Overwhelmed with his pain and confusion, I screamed and begged for mercy with him.

Whether that mercy was for him or for myself, I honestly didn't know. But I continued until my world fell apart and I eventually passed out from the empathetic overload.

I still felt that little boy deep within my soul, as if we'd remained connected—no matter the time or the distance. My heart whispered his name, when I chose to listen.

Rowan, it said.

Fantasy or reality? I had no way of knowing, but that was

what I called him when he visited me in the dreaming. A little boy lost in confusion and soaked in pain.

It was that event that had caused my parents to have me committed. I'd been sedated and placed in Dr. Hanley's *loving care* (cue sarcasm) and housed at his asylum. For years, I bounced around to various private institutions where the staff loved to remind me that I was less than nothing.

Once the will to live had been bled from my soul, I eagerly embraced death and ultimately died in the darkness of the asylum basement—alone and forsaken.

I FELT a small hand on my cheek and my eyes flew open in confusion. My nightmares followed me out of the dreaming and chased me into wakefulness.

"Don't cry, My Lady," Violet whispered.

Using my dragon essence for illumination, I saw Violet hovering in front of me. Her brows furrowed with distress and tears glistened in her expressive, purple eyes.

She flew forward again and this time gently gathered my tears into her hands, as if they were rare and treasured. She brought her cupped hands to her mouth and drank of their emotion. A precious, though painful, gift from my heart.

"I can't bear your pain, or Rowan's."

"You felt Rowan's pain? The little boy in my mind?" I asked surprised.

"Yes," Violet confessed, "I feel him whenever he visits you within the dreaming, but only when I'm as ink upon your skin."

"I wish I knew where he was and what happened to him. I thought he'd be in the Amulet of the Dead when I destroyed it, but I never found him."

"You will eventually, or at least I think so."

"When I think of Rowan, there's this pull within my soul —an undeniable need to run to him and rescue him from the hell he suffers."

"I know, My Lady. I can feel your need and the compulsion. I saw you tether him to your soul and I think that is why you feel so connected to him. Just like you dream and feel Aiden at times, they will remain a part of your soul until you decide to release them."

"You can see these memories as well as feel them?"

Violet bowed her head and simply replied, "Yes."

What more could I say to that, Violet had been a witness to all my nightmares and all of my demons—and yet, she was still here. I was blessed the day that I found her and every day thereafter, because she chose to stay with me.

Violet landed next to me and sat down on a pile of my hair. She wrapped some of the red strands around her neck, like a scarf. Baffled, I watched as she then picked up a chunk of my black hair to wrap around her shoulders, like a shawl.

She shrugged and tilted her delicate chin when she saw my expression and said, "I'm cold."

"How in the world did you get here?"

"I came with you when those Neanderthals took you from Everlasting. The shackles made me shift from your skin. I quickly grabbed ahold of your hair and hung on for dear life. The wind tried its best to pull the strands from my fingers. I couldn't reach your shoulder to lay upon your skin—the wind was too damned strong to move. I almost blew away with the force of it." She finished dramatically.

I could just imagine how hard that must have been for the delicate little faery.

"Lord, have mercy! I'm so glad that you're okay. Violet, I know the others can't see you, but I worry that they might sense you. Why in the world did you follow me?"

"How else would you get free? You're too stubborn to call for help."

"Pot and kettle."

"Hmmff!" She sassed me.

We were peas in a pod, as the saying went—destined to meet and fated to bond.

"What is going on, do you know?" Violet asked me.

"I don't know. They haven't really said anything. But I'm sure they will."

26

"Do you know why we took you from sanctuary?" Asked one of the three clansmen standing on the other side of the prison bars.

My cold stare conveyed what I wouldn't. I refused to acknowledge them or their questions. They would either tell me or they wouldn't. I knew how these games were played all too well.

We'd kept my past and all that I had endured, a secret from the clans so they had no idea who and what they were dealing with. I was horribly stubborn and more than a little determined to protect my family.

He continued to say, "It was for the protection of the dragon clans."

Thankfully, my musical shield had been reinforced before they arrived. They would have surely felt my incredulous emotions just then. These men couldn't be serious. All I wanted to do was protect the clans, that was the whole point of Everlasting—protection for all the clans.

I had to force myself not to respond to that or to roll my eyes or smile at Violet's mirth. She had shifted to ink when she'd felt the clansmen coming back to the cave and was on my side again. She always knew things before I did and would usually warn me, except this time she didn't.

I wondered why, but before I could ask her, the clansmen began again. They each took a turn talking *at* me.

"We don't trust you or your motives. All the clans are thankful they chose to wait to have their mated dragons come to Everlasting. We know what you're planning. We know from bitter experience, what your *kind* has done to ours over the centuries, and we won't stand for it," said the clansman to my right.

"We told the clan leaders all about you. They know exactly who and what you are, but they're blind where you're concerned. They believe you," he sneered, "are the clans' only hope. That you're the last true Phoenix spoken about in clan legend," the clansman on the left interjected, derision dripping from his tone, along with the spittle from his lips..

"You're not! Our clan legend would never have druid blood running through their dragon veins!" The last clansman screamed at me through the bars, "I see you're not denying it."

There's no way they could have known I'd smeared that

small amount of Hanley's druid blood across my glyph —no way.

"Tell us about your druid father and dragon mother. An affront and an abomination to all dragons."

This time the gasp escaped before I could censor it.

"Violet? How could they have discovered my secret? No one knows."

"You will never lead our people!" The center clansman screamed at me.

"DeChadik, it had to be. He was at the estate when you learned the truth about your parents. He must have overheard," Violet answered.

"Violet!" I yelled in alarm, *"He must know about Sterling. I have to warn him. He'll be blindsided. He won't be expecting an attack and I'm sure DeChadik is planning one. Oh, I should have confessed to him that I was Mia."*

Regret and remorse left a bitter taste in my mouth. By not confessing the truth to Sterling, my brother, I had betrayed him and our family and placed him in danger. Our parents would be ashamed, something I was all too familiar with.

"Violet, we have to warn Sterling. I'm going to drop my shield and try to connect with him. He's so hidden behind his own shield like I am, that he probably won't hear me.. No, I can't...I can't do that because my family will hear me and I won't put them in danger."

"Let me go to Sterling. I can do it and these buffoons will have no idea that I was ever here or that I'm leaving now."

"Please, Violet, would you go and warn him? But do not tell him where I am. And do not come back, little missy. I will not have you put yourself in danger for me."

She didn't respond except for a stinging sensation along my side, letting me know that she was moving.

"I mean it, Violet. Promise me that you will not endanger yourself!"

"I will do as you ask, My Lady."

"Thank you, my beautiful little sister."

"Thank you, My Lady, for loving me so well. You are the reason for my continued existence. My life is a debt that can never be repaid and I will be indebted for eternity and happily so. I will go now."

"Wait!"

But I was too late, as I could feel Violet shifting from my skin and in flagrant disregard of the three stooges screaming at me. She materialized on the other side of the bars and behind them.

She looked contemplative, as if weighing several different options before she curtsied midair, snapped her fingers and disappeared before my eyes. We'd been together for years now and I had no idea she could do that.

We all had secrets.

I was alone with the three men screaming at me for existing and for wanting to save the dragon race. I remained laying on the floor, just where they had dropped me earlier. I still couldn't move, but the effects of the Damascus were wearing off. It shouldn't be too much longer before I was able to at least sit up.

The left and right clansmen turned and walked out of the cave without even glancing in my direction. I was clearly less than nothing in their eyes—been there, done that, and I'd died in the process. Their opinion meant nothing to me. The only hold they had over me was the physical one of being captured and imprisoned behind Damascus steel bars.

Central gave me one last parting shot before he turned to leave, "Enjoy your victory while you can because once DeChadik returns, your silence will be at an end. He will most definitely see to that!"

27

Here I was again—waiting for my captors to remember me. The last time I'd been left waiting, Hanley had thrown me into the dank asylum basement—where I'd *died* waiting!

Not one of my better days and yet—it was. I'd become Renascent that fateful day.

Eventually I would come to realize the full potential of my Phoenix Dragon, but not before a complicated and confusing journey from there to here. Some moments and lessons had been more profound than others, but every one valuable in some way or another.

The transition wasn't painless but, along the way I discovered who and what I am—I found me.

The most astonishing and life altering moment had only come recently—my parents had loved and wanted me. Their love had created the last true Phoenix—their Mia.

"And that's why you must die."

I lifted my head and sat forward, away from the wall where I was sitting, to look towards the entrance from where DeChadik had spoken. He was leaning against the cave wall with a look of bored indifference. How had he heard me?

"Blood," he answered, "It all comes back to blood. I've had yours, so I know everything that you know."

Quickly, I tightened my shield making it impenetrable. I had to keep him out of my thoughts.

"I can feel you scrambling to kick me out, but it won't work. We're connected regardless of whether you want to be or not."

Filling my head with loud music, I hid behind a wall of distortion. When did he have access to my blood? I didn't give it to him, that's for sure. It was hard to think with the distortion screaming through my mind.

"I'll tell you a little secret and one guaranteed to make you abandon your defiance."

Hulbetto had licked the bloody sword dripping with my blood within that flipped memory.

"I've known who and what you are for some time."

That was just a horrible nightmare within the dreaming. It wasn't real—was it?

"Cipriano just happened to reach you before I had the chance."

Had he orchestrated the whole nightmare to gain access to my blood?

"Pay attention," he said, snapping his fingers.

Was DeChadik the Morpheus Dragon? No, he couldn't be. A vision of his clansmen and women hanging from the old Oak tree flashed through my mind. No, he wouldn't do that.

Sconces, scattered about the cave, sprung to life at his snapped command. They illuminated the cave in a soft, comforting glow that was at odds with the claustrophobic confinement of my cell and the hovering menace that he projected.

DeChadik had masqueraded as Hulbetto. He murdered his clan, but to what end? So that we'd stop wearing the amulets? Surely he wouldn't have done that. But, it just figures, I exchanged one anagram for another.

Hulbetto/DeChadik had licked my blood from the sword, that had really occurred. Just like the injuries I sustained— they were real and had hurt like hell.

The light caused DeChadik's blonde hair to glow with a halo, but the effect caused him to look more demonic, than angelic. When he turned in my direction, at first I thought he looked like Hulbetto, then morphed to look like Sebastian, my adoptive father.

I hadn't seen Sebastian in years, not since he and Helena had sent me back to Hanley and his asylum. They were under the impression I had died in a fire that swept through the institution.

I always planned to go back and check on them, just to see how they were doing. I don't know why, they couldn't have cared for me, considering they consigned me to the hell that was Hanley. If I manage to get out of this situation, I'll go find them, just to see that they are okay. I couldn't talk with them because they thought I was dead.

"You missed your chance. They're dead."

Breaking my silence, I whispered, "What?"

"I told you I'd win. I killed them years ago. Anything and everything connected to you will be eliminated!"

Snapping his fingers again, DeChadik proceeded to decimate my heart with the vision he played upon the cave wall. I couldn't escape it, even if I wanted to, but I deserved to be tortured. I believed Hanley and not Sebastian and Helena. They had truly loved me...

The vision was of Sebastian holding an unkempt Helena. I had never seen her in any way other than put together and beautiful. Her midnight-blue eyes were distraught and filled with tears, which flowed in a river unchecked down her pale cheeks. Sebastian's hair was more grey than brown now, and deep lines bracketed his solemn grey eyes and mouth, just like Helena's.

She looked so tiny in his arms, a shell of the vibrant, larger-than-life mother I remembered.

"I don't understand," she turned and cried against

Sebastian's chest, "how can she be alive? They told us she died in that damned asylum!"

"I don't know, love," Sebastian told her, pulling her tighter into his arms and against his chest.

Sebastian turned and looked away from her and addressed someone else in the room with them, "DeChadik, tell me what you know about our daughter and her whereabouts."

No, no, no! I was pleading in my mind knowing it was futile.

"She killed Hanley, her guards and all the other patients that became trapped by the fire she had set to cover her tracks. She's a mass murderer and has been on the run ever since. I work with the government that's been tracking her movements and we have noticed that she has been visiting your home routinely."

"What?" Sebastian exclaimed, "We haven't seen her at all. She has not been in contact with either one of us."

"That's good to know. We wondered if you might be aiding her in avoiding us and therefore, her capture and rightful punishment."

"We have not seen her since…since we took her back to Darren Hanley," Helena said. "Why did we do that, Sebastian?" she asked, sitting in his lap and looking into his equally confused eyes. "Why did we send her back? I know we didn't want to. We had decided to take care of her ourselves. We shouldn't have listened to Darren, he would be alive today and we would still have our daughter. Our Sarah, our beautiful Snow White."

She threw herself onto Sebastian sobbing, her delicate shoulders shaking with the force of her grief and remorse.

I could feel their emotions, despite this only being a vision, the residual pain was evident…

"We are worried for you and your wife's safety," DeChadik told them, as he walked into view, "which is what brought me here today. She's targeted you, that much is clear. Maybe she wants to make you pay for the abuse she suffered while at the asylum, but specifically at the hands of Hanley—he was the worst of the offenders. But surely, you must have known how he loved to abuse his patients, after all, you were on the board of directors."

Sebastian paled to a greyish-green and Helena sobbed as if her heart had truly just shattered.

"We would like to place you both in protective custody, so if you would gather your things and come with me, we can get the process started. We want to set a trap for your daughter here. She's a danger to herself and to the community at large, but especially to the both of you."

Sebastian looked resolved, standing to meet DeChadik eye-to-eye. I'd seen that look before and knew exactly what would happen next.

"No, we won't be going with you. If our daughter comes home, we will detain her here and then call the authorities. And this time, I will ensure that she gets the proper treatment and help that you say she needs. But we will wait here for her to arrive," he ended defiantly.

"That's unfortunate."

DeChadik transformed his hand into a dragon's claw and struck through Sebastian's chest. He was quick as a cobra and ripped Sebastian's heart out of his chest with a sucking sound.

He licked at the blood that pulsed from the still-beating heart, as Sebastian collapsed to the floor and Helena threw herself on top of him, clinging to her beloved.

I turned away from the look of sheer delight and euphoria

on DeChadik's face. The look of shock on Sebastian's face and the abject terror on Helena's because she knew she would be next. The horror continued...

DeChadik let my father's dead heart drop to the floor at his feet. Shifting to dragon, he set them ablaze with his dragon fire, then turned to shadow and left.

The knowledge that Hanley had controlled their minds so he could have what he had wanted—me, made my stomach turn over with nausea and my heart ache yet again, for all that was lost.

Helena's screams echoed through my mind long after the horrific vision had ended.

"And you shall die, just as she did, but you'll have no pyre to rest upon. No beloved to cling to as you scream your final breath. Have you ever had a lover, Phoenix? Anyone that would hold you as you die?"

I refused to speak.

"No? I wouldn't think so. Who would have you? Your blood is defiled and tainted by druid blood, making you an affront to the dragon race."

I was too lost within the darkness of my mind to pay attention to DeChadik, so I continued to ignore him. The sounds and images of Sebastian and Helena continued to haunt my mind. Vignettes from the vision flashed back-and-forth between their shocking defense of me and their ultimate deaths because of me.

More deaths to mark upon my soul.

The sound of Sebastian's defiance and Helena's love and

distress over sending me back to the asylum, would echo through me for centuries. As would the fact they died believing I was a monster capable of mass murder.

"Your brother will be next for the blood he shares with you. He cannot be allowed to live either."

"You need to get your facts straight, DeChadik. Charani's brothers are more than you can handle, I'd be running if I were you."

DeChadik spun quickly around to face Sterling.

"Ha!" DeChadik exclaimed, with a slight hitch in his voice. "That's rich. You don't even know the truth yet, do you?" He asked with smug condescension, recovering from his momentary surprise.

Oh God, I should have told him sooner.

"That..." DeChadik said, pointing to where I laid on the dirt floor behind the bars...

Frantically, I tried pushing my way through Sterling's shield to tell him first, but at this point, the damage of omission was done.

"...Is your sister."

Sterling looked at me in disbelief, confusion, and a dawning realization of the truth. We had the same crystal blue eyes and dark hair as our father.

Sterling charged DeChadik with no warning at all.

"I refuse to lose my sister. You. Will. Not. Win."

Each word was punctuated by Sterling's fist.

I was finally able to move, but trapped as I was behind these bars, I couldn't shift, so I was no help to my brother.

They were fighting hand-to-hand in human-form and from what I could tell, Sterling had the advantage. He was taller, quicker, and had more skill. All those months training the elite guard at Everlasting had not gone to waste.

DeChadik shifted to a smaller dragon and unleashed his dragon fire at Sterling and then at me, before fleeing from the cave.

Coward!

Dragon fire was clinging to whatever it had touched and filling the cave with smoke. I'd jumped out the way, missing his blast, but lucky for me, it had caused the bars to warp and bend enough that Sterling was able to pull me through to the other side.

Breathing was becoming difficult, but for a brief moment we each gazed upon our sibling, acknowledging the fact that we were family with our eyes alone. Sterling raised his hand to tuck my red Phoenix hair behind my ear and said, "Mia," as he did so.

"We have to go, Sterling. We can't let him escape."

"I know, let's go."

We ran out of the cave in pursuit of DeChadik. We needed to catch him before he could escape. Sterling shifted to shadow to travel faster through the tight and winding passageway. It was difficult to breathe and to see due to the thick smoke, so I followed his lead as shifting would alleviate both issues.

DeChadik had failed to kill me with his dragon fire, but the subsequent smoke tried its best to finish the job for him.

As Sterling and I breached the entrance of the cave, we shifted back to human to search for where DeChadik had gone.

"There he is," Sterling yelled, pointing towards the east.

We ran and dove off the bluff together.

Sterling threw his arms wide—relishing that moment of free-fall and shifted seamlessly to a Phoenix Dragon. Shocked by that revelation, my shift wasn't as smooth and momentarily slowed my pursuit.

I quickly caught up with Sterling and since we were in dragon-form, I spoke with him, mind-to-mind.

"Were you going to tell us you're a Phoenix?"

"Yes, when the time was right."

His scales were an unusual color, more green than dragon blue, with a pearlescent red hue to them.

DeChadik was ahead of us, but not by much. He must have felt us because he turned his head to see where we were. His dragon was blue, his scales a blend of pink and green; and, smaller than ours, probably because he wasn't a Phoenix and we were.

A crescent moon was hanging low in the night sky providing a bit of illumination, but too many shadows. Luckily, vision wasn't an issue when in dragon form. Dense fog was hovering over the ground and the waterways blanketed them in invisibility.

After flying in circles over the various bluffs, DeChadik dropped and disappeared below the fog. We pulled up and waited, knowing he would backtrack and attack swiftly.

I could feel Sterling's anger and need for vengeance.

Waves of sick anticipation slammed into me—the oily residue familiar, yet unrecognizable. I'd left my protective shield wide open to allow for a better connection to Sterling and to DeChadik. But connecting with DeChadik's emotions proved futile, as there were none—just a void of darkness.

"Do you feel that, Sterling?"

"I do."

Sterling was on my right and closer to the bluffs. DeChadik had been between us and ahead but was now below us somewhere—lurking.

"There's someone on the bluff, let's..."

Before I could finish, the unmistakable sound of a crossbow releasing, echoed through the air.

"Bank left! Bank left!"

The arrow missed Sterling's wing by a breath as he fell off, rolling to his left and directly into DeChadik's dragon fire. He pulled up, just as another arrow was released and then another—in rapid succession.

"The apprentice."

I was torn between fighting DeChadik and killing the apprentice, just as I knew Sterling was.

"You get DeChadik, I'm going after the apprentice for killing my parents. Our parents!" I told him, and took off.

Tucking in my wings, I flew straight at him, leaving Sterling to deal with DeChadik. It was his turn to be shocked and I could feel it reverberate through my wide open shield. He was torn between killing DeChadik and killing the apprentice.

"Mia?"

"Yes."

"We will talk about all of this later, Mia. Go get your man and I'll get mine!"

Sterling executed a perfect barrel roll and took off after DeChadik. He was bigger and faster. Once he caught up to him, they engaged in a fierce aerial dogfight and Sterling fired the first dragon fire volley straight at DeChadik.

Wishing him luck, I turned to find the apprentice. He was going down.

Or maybe I was, I thought frantically, as I maneuvered quickly to miss being skewered by another arrow.

No matter which direction I moved, the arrows tracked my movements, I was barely escaping their trajectory. They were fired at me, one after another, without much respite between releases. Some type of automatic quick-action release—I had no idea.

What I did know was that they were coming in—fast and heavy.

He remained hidden below the fog, but I had a general idea of where he must be, based on the trajectory of the arrows. I tried to fly around behind where they were firing, but the arrows followed me, tracking me through my movements.

I couldn't figure out how he was releasing the arrows so rapidly and was tired of dodging the deadly missiles, so I shifted to shadow and dropped to the bluffs below me. The arrows had ceased flying, for now.

He was nowhere that I could see, but the dense fog hid both of us. Shifting to human, I methodically searched the area for where he was hiding. I could feel his malice and smell the lingering dark magic, hanging suspended in the fog, making his location indeterminate.

He could be anywhere.

Stumbling around blind, I made my way towards where I

thought the den of the devil would be. It was difficult because the terrain was rugged with rocks, thick shrubs, and unfortunately for my skin, needle-sharp locust trees that loved to slice.

In the middle of a rare clearing sat a remote-triggered automatic crossbow machine, which explains how he had fired so rapidly. He could be anywhere in the area, even miles away. I felt him, but there was a barrier that hid his location.

Dark magic at work, no doubt.

I wasn't about to leave this crossbow machine here, armed and ready to kill my dragon brethren. I shifted to destroy it like I had Hulbetto's bloody cairn. To add height to my dragon weight, I rose high above the ground and dropped rapidly to destroy his weapon.

Hot, blinding pain ripped though my wing, as an arrow tore through it, leaving tiny fragments embedded within the scales and membrane. The force of the arrow flipped me away from the crossbow and I came down in human form. Rolling as I landed, I jumped up to face my attacker.

My arm was still bleeding, despite shifting. Damascus steel, the *kryptonite* of the dragon race.

The sound of running feet heralded the rapid approach of my nemesis, the apprentice. I wanted to kill the bastard, face-to-face, for what he did to my family.

I wish I could snap my fingers like Dreah and create a weapon, because I needed one—now. Shifting wasn't an option.

He slowed his approach, but walked into the clearing on the offensive. With determined strides and murder in his narrowed, black eyes, I was sent scrambling.

Reciting the spell Dreah had taught me, I snapped my fingers, opened my hand and—nothing.

Jumping over a rock that was determined to trip me, I tried again. I recited the words, snapped fingers, and opened my hand and—a wand-sized staff appeared.

Really?

I threw the wand at him, as he closed the distance between us, hitting him in the face, angering him even more and he charged at me.

It was like my little hatchling all over again because I didn't know what I was doing.

He swiped the staff at my feet. I jumped over it and pivoted mid-air to avoid being bashed in the head as I dropped back to the ground. Trying once more for a weapon to match his, I recited the words—again, snapped my fingers, and—a staff appeared in my awaiting hand.

Apparently the third time really is the charm, and timely, too!

Raising my staff, I was able to block the blow that was aimed at my head. We exchanged blows back and forth. I knew I wouldn't be able to keep this up for long; I could feel my blood dripping down my arm and it was becoming weaker.

"I take it your drampires never believed you were good

enough to join their ranks. Odd, I didn't think they were very discriminating," I said, attempting to distract and incite him.

"You know nothing, dragon!"

"I know you're a lowly apprentice."

Maybe I shouldn't have poked the bear.

He charged me with demented aggression using repetitive strikes that were difficult to counter. I was tiring and would have to do something soon or lose this battle.

I thrust my staff at him for a chest blow, spinning to jab at his kidneys, and jumping away from his return blows. He came at me, over and over, pushing me towards a collection of rocks. I didn't see them until it was too late.

I tripped and fell. My staff flew out of my hands as I lost my balance and fell onto a large boulder—eerily reminiscent of that damned bloody cairn. My attempt to jump was thwarted when he brought his staff to rest against my throat, pushing hard against my larynx.

Breathing and swallowing were extremely difficult as I was wedged against the boulder and couldn't escape the pressure. I tried to shift, but the residual Damascus arrow prevented me from doing so.

"I will hold you here, at my mercy, until DeChadik returns and we reap your Phoenix essence. Right here!"

He reached behind his back and pulled forward Dramascus shackles. If he managed to put those on me, I would have no way to defend myself.

The apprentice pulled the staff away from compressing my throat and inhaled deeply. I prepared for the blow...

"Be ready, My Lady!"

"Violet!"

Crazy faery, I told her not to come back. She threw some kind of powder into the apprentice's eyes and that's when I made my move.

Jumping up, I concentrated on changing just my hand into a dragon claw, like DeChadik did before killing Sebastian.

My hand didn't fully transition, but it was enough. I shoved my clawed hand deep into his chest and ripped out his heart.

Vengeance was mine!

Oh God, what have I done?

I thrust into the apprentice's mind, searching for anything about Aiden.

All I managed to feel were vague thoughts about Aiden from when he had stolen the Sword of Dramascus from Hulbetto's warehouse. There was nothing that pointed to where he could be.

I was a complete failure. In my blind need for vengeance, I forgot about Cipriano's search for the apprentice and Aiden would suffer for my selfishness.

How was I going to tell Cipriano that I killed the only person that could lead us to his brother?

I would face Cipriano and tell him what I had done, but for now I would help Sterling capture DeChadik. I still couldn't shift because of the arrow shrapnel scattered throughout my arm.

"Here, My Lady, I can help you with that," Violet said as she shifted off my skin.

"What did you throw in the apprentice's eyes?"

She looked at me and shrugged, "Faery dust."

"You risked exposure to help me. Are you in danger now, Violet?"

"All will be well, besides you are worth whatever minimal risk traveling to Faery may have caused."

We'd never discussed why she was hiding at Everlasting with us, but I knew that she was. She hid upon my skin to escape detection from those who would do her harm, or that's what I assumed she was doing. I didn't ask her about her demons and she didn't ask me about mine—we just acknowledged that they existed.

She waved her hands over my arm and slowly, but surely, the arrow bits and pieces were drawn out—to drop on the ground at my feet. I could feel the difference, the numbness and tingling receded and the bleeding slowed to a stop.

Damascus steel didn't bother Violet or others from Faery. However, she couldn't tolerate iron, specifically cold-forged iron. It was made without the heat of a forge and therefore, very difficult to make. It was her kryptonite, just like Damascus was mine.

Shifting to my dragon, I stretched my wings, feeling a slight pinch as they continued to repair themselves. I turned my dragon head towards the apprentice and unleashed my dragon fire to take care of his remains.

Ashes to ashes and now, dust upon the wind.

"Come, Violet, let's go take care of DeChadik."

She transitioned onto my skin, just as I launched from the bluff to rise above the fog. I immediately saw Sterling, but he was alone.

"Where's DeChadik?"

"I have no idea, he just disappeared," he told me, confused. *"We were grappling mid-air. I'd scored some significant hits and he was bleeding profusely. He was showing signs of fatigue so I thought he'd be forced to shift and we'd take our fight to the ground."*

"Then where could he have gone?"

"He slipped from my claws to drop below the fog and disappeared. I've been searching for him."

"He's a Chameleon Dragon. I discovered his ability when I was in the cave, so he could have been right in front of you and you wouldn't have seen him."

Sterling said something under his breath and in a language I didn't understand, but the meaning was not lost on me.

"My sentiments exactly. We should head back to Everlasting to warn everyone."

"What happened with the apprentice?"

"He's dead."

"Well done. He deserved it for destroying our family."

"But, I screwed up, Sterling," I couldn't keep the pain from my voice and didn't bother trying, *"I forgot about Aiden,"* I confessed.

We still hadn't spoken about the fact we were siblings or about our lives to date. What must he think of me now?

"I think you are beautiful and courageous, Mia."

"But, I didn't tell Cipriano about you. I didn't tell him about Kristóf and Júlia, I wanted to mourn them first."

"I would have done the same and Cipriano will understand."

"He won't, Sterling, you don't understand. It's Aiden that I'm destroyed over. Cipriano has been searching for centuries to find his brother and I just killed the only man who might have information about where he could be located."

"Explain."

"We don't share this, but Aiden was trapped by dramperic dark magic within the Sword of Dramascus. He's been forced to kill our brethren for centuries. Hulbetto used Aiden to mortally injure our father which led to his death and Júlia's. He used Aiden to mortally injure me."

"Mia, will you tell me about you? If you do that, I think the rest will make sense to me."

We spent the rest of the trip to Everlasting discussing our pasts. I started with the vision Dreah had shared with us and how Sebastian and Helena had come to adopt me. I told him about my life with them.

"It was so confusing as a child, to hear so many voices and to feel their pain. I was empathic, but I had no idea why. The little boy, Rowan, was my breaking point. His pain and cries for mercy had caused an empathic overload. My parents had been instructed to have me admitted to an asylum. I had no idea who or what I was at the time and I wouldn't fully understand it for years to come. But, it was the beginning of my journey to discovering the real me."

I shared most of my experiences from the asylum, but left out the most heinous of the experiments. He didn't need to know about those, there was no sense making him feel sorry for me and the pain I'd suffered. I couldn't stand to see, nor feel, his pity.

Sterling asked numerous questions and I, for the most

part, answered him truthfully. I explained about Dr. Hanley, his botched reaping, and discovering that Mia, the voice in my head was actually me. I told how Cipriano came to find me in my dungeon hell; that the stories he had shared with me had saved my mind and, his essence had saved my soul.

"I'm so thankful Cipriano found you and saved your life. I'm indebted to him for making you Renascent and will strive to find a way to repay him. We would have never known each other..." he trailed off, as all the *what-ifs* floated through our minds.

The fog hovering over the serpentine Lake of the Ozarks had lifted to reveal the Magic Dragon. The surface tonight was glassy in its stillness and kissed by the crescent moon. I looked down to see our reflections captured upon the mirror-like surface as we traveled the waterways to home.

Finishing my story, I told him about finding Dreah and Aiden at Hulbetto's warehouse.

"Aiden had begged me, 'Tell my brother to break the sword and destroy me! I can no longer endure the blood of our race upon my hands and staining my soul.' I could feel Aiden's lingering sense of desolation, but before that feeling could disappear, along with Aiden, I snatched a remnant of his essence and tethered it to my soul for safekeeping. We will find him, but I refuse to destroy him."

"That is how I will repay Cipriano. I will join in the search for Aiden."

Turning to look at Sterling, I was saddened by all the time we had lost. What might our lives have been like had we not been separated?

I ended this part of my life by explaining how the other voices in my head belonged to the collective, which were thousands of our brethren that had been trapped in the Amulet of the Dead, and my coalescence with them.

"They saved my life when I was mortally wounded by Hulbetto and, along with Mia, helped me to realize the full potential of my Phoenix. Together, we destroyed Hulbetto."

"You are a warrior, Mia. As the last true Phoenix, you were born to lead the dragons. Once they realize who and what you are, there will be no question as to your rightful place as clan leader to all the dragons at Everlasting."

"Sterling, you're the eldest and as such, you should be the rightful leader. You're a Phoenix, too."

"But, I'm not a true Phoenix. I wasn't born dragon, but rather druid. Júlia gifted me with her dragon essence after I died from a childhood illness and I became Renascent and as such, dragon. Eventually, I became Phoenix when I shifted for the first time and survived, just like you. Though unlike you, I knew what to expect and had Kristóf and Júlia to aid me in my transition."

After that astounding revelation, the rest of the trip was made in comfortable silence. I didn't share with Sterling the revelations DeChadik had made regarding Sebastian and Helena.

How much had he'd seen, I wondered, but decided no one could help me with the pain or the guilt I felt, so it didn't matter if he knew or not.

Could I have saved them from DeChadik if I had returned

home to see them? I'll never know and I now must live with the knowledge that they had truly loved me and died believing me a monster.

I summoned the elite guard to come to the Great Room for a debriefing regarding DeChadik and all that had transpired. Tarrin and Tauric were the first to arrive, but once the entire elite guard was there, I shared most of what had happened. When I finished, hellfire was blazing in their eyes and retribution was in their battle cry.

They would be a force to reckon with.

"I'm calling an emergency meeting with the remaining clan leaders and would like you to be present," I asked, though it came out sounding like a question.

"There's no place we'd rather be than right here, protecting the leader of Everlasting," Eduard, their elected captain, said.

As one, the guard proceeded to take to a bended knee—heads bowed and fists over hearts, in a show of solidarity and united in their fealty to me, the last true Phoenix.

It was humbling to see their show of support and unequivocal loyalty. I would do everything within my power to maintain that trust.

This morning's meeting should be interesting, though I feared it would not go as smooth as this one and would contain far less acceptance.

Tarrin and Tauric wanted to speak with me privately. Before the guard left, they assured me they would return before the meeting started and left to have breakfast at the garrison. Miss Janna had taken charge of feeding them.

"We know you're in good hands." Delia, one of the women elite guards said, with a wink. "Miss Janna said she was making scones with clotted cream. You can't miss out on her scones, so I'll bring you back a plate."

"Thank you, Delia, I would never, ever turn down scones with clotted cream."

Once I was alone with the twins, Tarrin walked over to me and pulled me into his arms.

"Why in the hell didn't you reach out to us, Charani?"

Pulled from his embrace, Tauric hugged me tight and admonished, "You do not have to be so strong all the time. We are family, Sister, and you should remember that the next time you find yourself in trouble."

"I know, but I didn't want to endanger you—any of you. I would never recover from such a loss, especially if it were somehow my fault."

"Ian and Isabella will be here shortly," Tarrin told me,

"They're family and need to be here. Isabella should be surrounded by protection, especially now. Dreah is still with the witches and safe in their care, but I don't trust DeChadik.

"Thank you. They were next on my list of things to do. They shouldn't be alone just now. I know they wanted some peace and quiet, however, I fear that will be hard to find in the days to come."

"WE'VE GATHERED HERE today for a multitude of reasons. It's imperative that we improve communications between each clan. We must step past these insular ways of centuries past and embrace a new way of life.

"We cannot afford to sit in isolation while our race is decimated—from within and from outside. The best way to destroy any culture, plus undermine what we are attempting to establish here at Everlasting—is from the inside. DeChadik was quite adept at doing just that."

I'd called for an emergency meeting with all the clan leaders that had remained at Everlasting—some had left in the wake of my abduction and the subsequent fallout. DeChadik had been fairly thorough in his objective to further fracture the clans by sowing the seeds of distrust and dissension.

"With his affable façade, DeChadik hid the true nature of his personality—a cold-hearted psychopath—a rare

Morpheus and Chameleon Dragon, changeable and deadly. He'd used this combination to systematically reap the essence and power from his own dragon brethren. And he would have ultimately decimated our entire culture had we not figured out what he was doing and how.

"I'm not sure I can prove it, but I'm positive he killed his own clansmen. What better way to cast doubt upon the usefulness of the amulets than to kill his people with the very amulets meant to protect them. I clearly angered him by gifting the protective amulets to everyone, but they are just as effective as we thought they'd be and prevented him from invading your dreams.

"As you should all know by now, I, Charani, am the last true Phoenix Dragon. I recently discovered my true birthright and I've finally accepted that truth. What I'd like to do is create a roundtable counsel. This counsel would act together and on behalf of all the clans—acting as one governing body. What I'm hoping is that we can guide our clansmen through the upcoming changes and into a brighter future."

"Where is Cipriano? He should be the one here and leading us," Geoffrey said.

"Cipriano is right where he should be, searching for his brother, and we will leave him to it," I stated, my words clipped and precise.

"Charani is the rightful leader of Everlasting and if you and your clansmen don't like it, Geoffrey—take them and leave!"

"Thank you, Sterling," I said.

He was my brother and I could see that he was going to take that duty seriously.

"Geoffrey, I'm done fighting for your approval and acceptance. I am who I am. If you cannot accept this, then I will suggest that you leave, though I would hate to see more clansmen murdered by DeChadik and his minions."

After that verbal throw-down, the meeting progressed better than I expected. Ultimately, those clan leaders that had stayed at Everlasting after my abduction remained—including Geoffrey. He and the other leaders saw the wisdom of fighting our enemy together, instead of separately.

Most of the clans that had left, returned after the elite guard explained to them all that had occurred with DeChadik's attempt to destroy Everlasting and the dragon race as a whole. They were alarmed, as they should be, that he was still at large and that we remained in danger.

I should have realized sooner how the dragon deaths were occurring, but hindsight was always too clear. If I had not been captured by DeChadik and the others, we might still be in the dark and blind to the truth.

DeChadik had been leading and directing the drampires in their assault against the dragons for centuries. Eventually, he would have succeeded in destroying our entire race, as well as steal the power from all those dragons.

But to what end?

What would he gain by being the last dragon standing?

What did he plan to do then? Without a mate, he couldn't produce offspring. Without dragons to rule, what was the point?

I would never understand—even if someone explained his motivations in simple terms, I couldn't comprehend killing just to have more power.

Despite recent events, some of the clans had decided, in the interest of safety and protection in numbers, to bring their mated dragons here. Every clansman at Everlasting was committed to the protection of these mated dragons and their offspring, should they be blessed, like Ian and Isabella.

So many things had happened and all at once, but acceptance of who and what I was had finally settled in—for all of us.

I really was the last true Phoenix.

3 2

History, whether in oral-form or written-form, is necessary, even paramount to the foundation of every society and we were no different. Our natural history was lost to us and we suffered in its absence.

At some point, in the distant past, we know that druid and dragon had mated and lived together in harmony. A relationship that was symbiotic, rather than parasitic, like what exists now between the druid-turned-drampire and dragon.

Our history had been buried by DeChadik as he strove to destroy all things Phoenix. He methodically turned the new generation of druid against dragon. He empowered them with the knowledge of how to steal our dragon essence to obtain their own, hijacked immortality.

He started by killing all dragons with knowledge about *true* Phoenix history. DeChadik wanted to be the only one left with this information. However, while there were many

Phoenix Dragons, like Cipriano and Ian, there was only one true Phoenix—me.

As the daughter of a druid father and a dragon mother—a true Phoenix, I was the only one known to be in existence.

Counter to what we assumed about our dragon history, these were shocking realizations and would take time to assimilate the implications. There could be druids out there waiting to be found by their dragon mates. This could change the very fabric and trajectory of our culture.

This could be the renascence of our race.

The clan leaders were having the hardest time with how they and their clans had been repeatedly manipulated. They had to alter their way of thinking, as it pertained to the druids and what joining with them could mean for our races. I wasn't centuries old, so for me it wasn't an adjustment.

Sterling told me the story of how Kristóf and Júlia first met. They had both felt that instantaneous connection that only mates experience and were completely confused, but there was no denying that visceral reaction.

Through their bravery and acceptance of what seemed taboo, they fell in love and stumbled upon the secret of dragon and druid history—we could be mated and have children, true Phoenix children.

Sterling, and their entire clan, had kept their mating a secret. Though, the clan did not realize that Júlia was with child when they went missing. Sterling had suspected it was a possibility and had searched endlessly for his sibling, knowing Kristóf and Júlia were already dead and would want me protected within the clan.

What settled my soul and brought peace to my heart, was the fact that I had been loved and wanted by my parents. They knew what I would mean for the dragon culture.

I was not a little girl thrown away.

Sterling, my brother. He had rescued me from my prison cave, thanks to Violet's intervention. He was a wonderful discovery and we were getting to know each other.

I was well and truly loved.

Cipriano had returned when he felt my distress, which doubled my guilt. I took him from his mission to find Aiden.

"I have so many things to tell you, but first, I killed the apprentice," I confessed quickly.

I refused to look away from his grey eyes allowing him to see my pain and remorse. I couldn't control the wayward tear that slipped free of my control to slide down my cheek.

"I would have done the same," he said, gently wiping the tear from my face, "He caused you so much harm."

"But that's just it, he did so much more than that."

I told Cipriano everything. All about Sterling and Kristóf and Júlia. I brought him up-to-date on everything surrounding DeChadik, including what he had showed me in the cave.

"Do you think that really happened? Or was he manipulating a vision of them to hurt me?"

"We will go and check on them to see if they are still alive.

He may have been toying with your emotions to make you suffer before he thought you would die. I wouldn't believe it, not yet, but prepare for the reality that it was indeed true."

My family, including Sterling, were all gathered for a private dinner. I wanted to tell them the story about my parents, Kristóf and Júlia, and, if Sterling was willing, I wanted him to share his story. I hoped he would include what he knew about druids and dragons mating.

Our father had been a druid until he'd met Júlia and they realized they were mated. After their bond was forged, he became dragon, too, sharing in her abilities. It was truly remarkable and I knew this would be the key to our future.

"Sterling," Dreah said as she came bouncing in the room, "I made you a special amulet that's just for family. But there's a process to it and we all have to be here to participate. So after dinner, we will finish this, okay?"

Sterling looked dumbstruck with what to say, "Thank you, little one..."

"Not you, too!" Dreah said with a roll of her eyes.

Laughing, Sterling said, "Yup, me too. Thank you for including me in your family."

"We chose our own family, Sterling, it's tradition. And we've all chosen you. So now you're stuck with all of us," Dreah said with a huge grin.

Ian strode quickly into our family's Great Room, concern evident on his face and in his voice, "Sister, have you seen Isabella?"

"She was nauseous and wanted some fresh air. She just stepped through the doors right there only a few moments ago," I told him, pointing to the french doors that led to the enclosed garden.

Isabella had been fighting nausea this whole pregnancy and still had a couple of months before their baby was due to be delivered. Their child would be first dragon since me and hopefully the start for a new generation of dragons.

"Something doesn't feel right," Ian replied, "I..." he stuttered, "I can't feel her," he said, running out the french doors to look in the garden.

Dropping my shield, I reached out, searching for Isabella and found nothing.

"Do you feel her, Violet?"

I felt Violet move along my side and I was jolted by a wave of terror, just before she exclaimed:

"My Lady!"

THE END

ENJOY THIS BOOK?

Enjoy this book?

You have the power to make a huge difference...

Reviews are so important in providing social proof, especially for other readers who may not know about my books. I don't have the resources of the big publishing houses to do extensive advertising, but I have something better...I have You!

A Loyal Reader.

If you've enjoyed this book, then I'd be grateful if you could take a few moments of your time to leave an honest review on this books Amazon page. Reviews help bring my books to the attention of other readers.

Review Coalesce

http://maxandren.com/max-andren-links/

Thank You in advance.

Max

Thank you for picking up Coalesce, a book in the Phoenix Dragon Collection! Not only did you read my book and my words, but you're taking the time to read this note as well. I'm truly humbled.

I've wanted to write for more years than I care to admit, but in 2014 I finally began this journey—at long last! Thank you for joining me as I travel down the many roads of my imagination.

People talk about writing and being a writer, as a solitary endeavor, but I don't see it as such because I have all of you walking beside me.

I hope that in some small way, my stories will touch your life

and you will come back for more—Because Do I Ever
Have More.

Follow Max on Amazon

https://www.amazon.com/
Max-Andren/e/B076CL2ZKK

Thank you,
Max Andren

ALSO BY MAX ANDREN

Urban Fantasy

A Phoenix Dragon Novel 01: Renascent

A Phoenix Dragon Novel 02: Coalesce

A Phoenix Dragon Novel 03: Everlasting—Coming Soon

ABOUT MAX ANDREN

Max Andren writes Fantasy and Urban Fantasy and her first novel, Renascent, was featured in a USA Today Bestselling anthology.

The Phoenix Dragon Collection: Renascent, Coalesce, and Everlasting are the first books on her journey and the foundation for the world she's creating.

She started her professional career as a Registered Nurse in a Pediatric Intensive Care Unit. She continued in school to become a Nurse Anesthetist. She still works in the medical field today but writes every day and night.

Max was born in the Midwest, but raised in Southern California. She's living back in the Midwest with her husband, their son and daughter-in-law, and their 10 year old Shih Tzu, Meme.

Be sure to sign up for her newsletter for New Release Notifications. No Spamming. No Promotions, just an email about upcoming releases.
Sign Up
Max Andren: Magic and Mythos.

http://maxandren.com/magic-and-mythos-book-link/

www.maxandren.com
maxandren@maxandren.com